TOXIC BLONDE

DAVID STEVER

Cinder Path Press, LLC

Cinder Path Press, LLC
5319 Tarkington Pl.
Columbia, MD 21044
www.davidstever.com

Cover Design: Brandi McCann/ebook-coverdesigns.com
Cover Photograph: Remy Musser/Shutterstock
ISBN: 978-09983371-2-8 (paperback)
ISBN: 978-09983371-3-5 (ebook)
Printed in the United States of America

To my parents,
Evelyn and George Stever,
with love

1

Two people having sex make all kinds of different noises and I have listened to them all in my years of investigative eavesdropping. Giggles, laughs, cries, sighs, whispers, gasps, screams, moans, groans, and grunts. I waited until Wallace Forman let out one last grunt—to give him one last moment of pleasure—before I destroyed his day. I removed my earpiece and set it on the hotel bed and turned off the receiver. I left Room 302, walked the six feet to Room 304, and pounded on the door.

"Mr. Forman?" Silence on the other side. I banged again.

A few moments passed and the door opened a crack. A man peeked through as I held up my old police badge. He had on trousers and an undershirt. The security chain went taut.

"What is it?"

"We need to talk, Wallace."

"How do you know my name?"

"I know everything. You are Wallace Forman of Forman/Roberts Insurance and your friend in there is Brittany Grimes. You are sixty-three years old, married to Elizabeth. She hired me to help you out of this situation. How about I come in?"

"No. Who are you?"

"Right now I'm your best friend. Trust me."

I watched his eyes give me the once-over. "I'm calling the police."

"You can do that, but before you do, ask Brittany about Valerie Kinney and Marie Marshall."

"What?"

"Valerie Kinney and Marie Marshall. Ask her."

He closed the door and their muffled voices went back and forth. I put my ear to the door but couldn't decipher anything. Less than a minute went by and the door cracked again.

"She doesn't know what you're talking about. We're calling hotel security."

"In my hand are copies of two felony warrants she has outstanding. Los Angeles and Phoenix. Wanted for fraud and extortion." The door closed and the voices went back and forth again. This time the door opened and he stepped into the hall.

"Who are you again?"

"Name's Delarosa. Private investigator." I held my identification in front of his face and then handed him the warrants. "She is Valerie Kinney on one, Marie Marshall on the other. Elizabeth hired me two weeks ago to follow you and investigate your friend."

His thin chest heaved hard with each breath. "Why should I believe you? Next you're going to want money. This is a shakedown."

"Mr. Forman, the shakedown is tucked between the sheets in there. She's a grifter, a con. How much did you give her in the past three months?" His brow furrowed and his eyes went to the floor. "Let's go in."

"Elizabeth knows?"

I nodded. "Your partner, too."

"Rick? Oh, Jesus."

"Why don't we go in the room so we can talk this through and come to a resolution?"

His hand shook as he opened the door. I followed him inside.

Brittany was in the bed with a sheet pulled up to her neck. "Wally, you let him in?"

"Everyone found out."

"What? Who is everyone?"

"Elizabeth, Rick."

"Oh my God. So, so what? They'll need to accept who we are and our relationship."

"It won't be that easy." He put a hand against the wall to steady himself. The color drained from his face. He shuffled a few steps to the bed and plopped down hard. His soft, doughy body was a rumpled lump on the corner of the bed. His faded white undershirt matched the gray of his hair, and his round belly bulged out on his lap.

"File for divorce. End it, baby. That's what we want, anyhow," she said. He sat staring at the floor. "Wally?"

"Why don't you put your clothes on and I'll tell you how this is going to go," I said.

"You're going to tell us?" Brittany asked. "Why don't you go to hell? Get out of our room. Wally, make him leave." He was silent and probably in shock. "Wally?"

Over the past two weeks, I observed and photographed Wallace and Brittany AKA Valerie AKA Marie checking in to motels and hotels, going to lunch and dinners, and walking the streets of the city. He moved around with Brittany on his arm and his chest puffed out with the bravado of a sixty-three year old man who is sleeping with a woman twenty-five years his junior. Now the realization of his embarrassing indiscretion crashed in on him.

I focused on the felon in the bed. "Get dressed."

"How about you mind your own business and get out?"

"Miss Grimes, or whoever you are, the sugar daddy well is dry from this point forward. You have two choices: deal with me, or I call the cops." I stepped back and leaned against the hotel room door. I couldn't chance her getting past me.

Wally finally spoke up, "Do as he says."

Her face flushed. "I don't believe this." She looked at me. "Are you going to leave?"

"Nope."

"Oh, I see. You want a peek, is that it? You want a free show? Okay, here you go." She threw off the sheet and hopped out of the bed. She thrust her arms in the air and twirled around. "Take a picture, you pervert."

"Stop it, Brittany," Wally snapped at her.

She had an extra fifteen middle-age pounds around her waist and hips and her pancake breasts were past their perky prime.

"Fine." She scooped up her clothes, stormed into the bathroom and slammed the door.

He stood and pulled on a shirt. "Not my finest moment, huh? Deep down, I knew it would not last. I knew...I knew she wanted money...I liked it...made me feel like a man again."

"It happens," I said. "We lose our minds when a female shows a little attention."

"I thought..." He sat back down on the bed. "It doesn't matter what I thought."

The bathroom door flung open and Brittany came out. "Let's go." She grabbed her purse and faced me. "Move out of our way."

I pulled a check and a sheet of paper from my pocket. "This is made out to you in the amount of ten thousand dollars. A little generous if you ask me, but it's from Elizabeth Forman." I held up the one-sheet contract and a pen. "If you take the money, you agree to leave Port City and never return. You also agree to cease all contact with Wallace and his firm. Forever."

She contemplated the offer for all of three seconds, huffed, grabbed the contract and pen from my hand, scribbled a signature, crumpled the paper into a ball and threw it across the room. I gave her the check and she split. She never once looked at Wallace.

I picked up the wad of paper and made an effort at smoothing it out. I took my transmitter—a bug—from behind the headboard where I placed it earlier in the day when the lovebirds went to lunch.

"You were listening?"

"Sorry."

"Why?"

"Photographs and recordings go a long way in a divorce settlement."

"How did you get in our room?"

"Cash in the hand is still king, Mr. Forman. Gather your things. I'm next door in 302."

I went to my room and tucked the transmitter and receiver into my attaché. Wallace walked in after a minute and appeared to be half the man who I had watched parade around town with his mistress on his arm.

"You get off doing this? Listening, watching; destroying people's lives?"

I faced him and was six inches taller, with a lot more muscle. "I'll pretend you didn't say that."

He sat down on the bed with his chin on his chest. "Now what?"

"You go back, ask for forgiveness. Tell them you temporarily lost your mind."

"Easy for you to say. What about the pictures and recordings?"

"They belong to your wife, but I think she wants this behind you. I've been at this work a long time and have seen many men in the same spot you're in now.

You're not the first, won't be the last. You'll be fine." I opened the door and he stood.

He had tears in his eyes.

"What a fool I am. She didn't even say anything. I trusted her."

I put my hand on his shoulder. "Love can be cruel, Wallace. Love can be cruel."

***

I called Jim Rosswell, my attorney friend, the one who funnels me business, and told him the Forman job was done.

"How'd he take it?"

"Humiliated. He'll get over it."

"Yep, we all do. Come by my office tomorrow at one. I have another job for you."

"What?"

"What you're good at. Cheating spouses."

"Jim, c'mon..."

"Be here at one. Trust me, nice price tag." He hung up.

Cheating spouse cases are routine, boring, and never pleasant. I peek into people's lives when they are less than their best and it is always two people doing something they should not, and that never leads to a happily ever after.

But in the words of a wise old private eye somewhere:

Infidelity pays the bills.

2

"Want some lunch?" Katie asked.

"Yes, thank you. Any excuse to get out of this store-room." The least favorite part of my duties as half-owner of McNally's Irish Pub: inventory. My partner, Mike as in Mike McNally, took care of the front of the house while I tended to the back. That was our deal, unless a PI job came my way, and that well has been dry for a while, except for last two weeks of tailing a philandering husband.

The twelve cases of liquor will have to wait to be opened, sorted, counted, and logged into our new computerized inventory tracking system. The old fashioned way of paper and pencil was fine by me, but our new hire, Katie Pitts—our part-time bartender, bookkeeper, waitress, my research assistant, and apprentice private investigator—insisted we upgrade to the modern era and arranged for a restaurant point-of-sale computer system. When it was first installed, it took me ten minutes to figure out how to sell a guy a draft beer.

Katie set a fancy-looking sandwich in front of me as I slid into my office/booth in the rear of the bar.

"What's this?"

"Gourmet grilled cheese," she said, with her hands on her hips.

"Kind of fancy for us."

"No. Artisan bread with cheddar cheese and sliced apple. We need to upgrade this menu if we expect to compete with other places in town. We can't keep serving hot dogs and wings."

"We're a bar. People come in here wanting to drink beer and eat bar food."

She sat opposite me and leveled her blue eyes. "We upgrade the menu, we upgrade the clientele."

"We don't need to upgrade the clientele. Cops and firefighters suit us fine."

"There are thousands of people in this city who should know about us. We're a cool bar and we're missing out on a lot of business." She got up from the booth. "Eat the sandwich." She went back to the kitchen and her food experiments.

I took a bite as Mike walked over with a beer for me. "Did she make you one of those? Out of this world, right?"

"Are you buying in to this new menu and all these new plans to attract more customers?"

"She's right. We haven't changed the menu since we opened. I've been frying the same chicken wings for six years. Maybe we should upgrade? Advertise some more. This place is a ghost town some nights. Happy hour crowd, then nothing."

I ate half the sandwich, and as much as I did not want to admit, it was delicious. "Who's going to cook if she's not here?"

"Me and Carlos, as long as the dish is not too complicated."

Katie returned to the booth and sat. "Liked it, didn't you?"

"Yes, I did, but we're not a gourmet joint," I said.

"C'mon, Johnny? There's incredible potential here."

Mike jumped in. "Here's the deal. I like the idea of a new look, changing a few things, liven it up. Why don't you put together some type of formal presentation and we'll decide?"

Katie turned to me.

"Seems reasonable," I said.

"Yes! I'm stoked. Thank you. This place will be so bangin' you'll be amazed. I'll start as soon as I get back from my vacation."

"Vacation?" I finished off the sandwich.

"Yes. My trip to San Juan. In five days."

"I don't remember anything about a vacation. Mike, do you remember anything about Katie going on vacation?"

"Don't leave me shorthanded for a week." He pointed to her. "Make sure your shifts are covered." Mike lumbered to the bar. "I have a restaurant to clean."

"Are you happy now?" I washed down the sandwich with my beer.

"Yes. But there's something else I want to ask you."

I peered at her over the lip of the bottle.

"I want to learn to shoot," she said.

"Not this again."

"Johnny, please...you said you would teach me."

"Those cases of liquor won't count themselves." I left the booth and she followed me to the storeroom.

"Why not? I want to learn. I should learn. Then I can get my carry permit."

I still see her duct-taped to a folding chair, sitting in the center aisle of a warehouse, wearing nothing but her underwear. Distressed, tired, panicked, but tough and resilient. Two maintenance workers abducted her after she played tennis and held her for ransom. Her father hired me to find her and bring her home—which I did. A few days later, she talked her way into working for us in the bar, and doing investigative background research for me. Even though she never stops talking, we love having her around. And not just for her tall, shapely body, long mane of blonde hair, and killer eyes—she just grew on us. Call it paternal. She is smart, resourceful, mature beyond her years, plus she knows how to work the damn computer.

"I told you I would teach you. I think everyone should learn how to handle a gun. But a conceal and carry permit is not necessary."

"So, you don't want me to be able to defend myself."

"Of course I do." I grabbed my box cutter and sliced off the top of the first carton. I recorded the count on the inventory sheet. She huffed and leaned in the doorway with her lips in a pout and her arms folded across her chest. I cocked an eyebrow. "That won't work."

"I want my PI license and having a permit is essential to my job."

"Nice try." The alarm on my cell phone chirped. "I have an appointment with Jim in thirty minutes."

"Does he have another job?"

"Yep."

"When were you going to tell me? I'll grab my notebook."

"No. I'm going. You finish this inventory and clean the kitchen before Mike gets his Irish up. We'll meet later this afternoon. And...and, when you come back from your trip, I'll take you to the range."

She threw a hug around me. I'm too easy.

3

The twenty-minute drive to Jim Rosswell's office took forty minutes in stop-and-go traffic. The offices of Rosswell-Ward, Attorneys at Law, were on the fourteenth floor of a twenty-five story modern glass and steel building that hovered over the Port City harbor. I parked in the building's underground lot. The elevator opened to his suite and Jim's assistant, Patty, ushered me back.

Rosswell-Ward is best described as a boutique firm catering to a roster of well-heeled entrepreneurs. Jim Rosswell made a small fortune taking companies public, becoming one of the country's foremost legal experts in IPO offerings and SEC regulations—and how to skirt them. Now, fifteen years later, Jim limits his personal practice to a select few clients. Most of the work he parcels out to me are background investigations of prospective corporate executives. Tedious and routine, but I can bill what I want. In the world of six-figure employment contracts, a few thousand on a background check is a nominal cost for a company, and easy paydays for me. The business climate in Port City enjoyed a steady growth over the past decade, due to our working harbor and the ancillary businesses it spawns. The major transportation companies in the country all maintain a presence in the city. So, Jim, and his reputation, are good for my business.

Patty parked me in a glass walled conference room. One wall overlooked the harbor, and the other wall had a view into the office suite. I waited fifteen minutes before he came in.

"Johnny, sorry to keep you. Thanks for coming." He was tall, slim, permanently tan, with a full head of thick, silver hair. "First, how's the beach house?"

"Lots of fix-up, cleanup, but I need the exercise."

"At least Kelly was cooperative. My second divorce, from Candice, was a nightmare. I'm still paying for it. You want a drink?" He took a bottle and two glasses out of a credenza and poured two short bourbons.

A month ago, Jim handled the legal work when I bought out my ex-wife's half of a beach cottage we co-owned. "I'm going to make it my hideaway. Maybe move out there someday."

"Beach hideaway—I need one of those. I got my eye on a pretty little associate we hired right out of law school. She says I'm her mentor." He handed me a glass.

"Don't crush her dreams too fast."

"All part of her education."

"Uh, huh."

"Down to business. I have client who suspects her husband of cheating. If he is, she'll ask for a divorce."

"You're doing divorce work?"

"Only as a favor. We went to high school together. Families are old friends. Here's the thing—the husband's loaded. So if she wants to go through with a divorce, the negotiations could be endless," he said.

"And the billing hours."

"Right. Even with my discount, it will be nice. Strictly pro-bono for now, except for your fee, until we figure out what the husband is up to. Your schedule clear?"

"Wide open."

"Perfect. Are you familiar with BST—Bellamy Space Technologies?" He finished off his bourbon in one gulp and poured himself another.

"Defense contractor?"

"Yes. Out in the Cameron Road Business Complex. Owned by one Thomas Bellamy."

"Seen his name in the paper a few times. Charity events and such."

"He started the company fifteen years ago after making a name for himself in the aerospace community. Developed state-of-the-art technology for GPS guidance systems. Went out on his own, landed a couple of sweet government contracts, and he's off and running. BST now manufactures navigational components for US military satellites."

"A sex scandal involving the CEO of a top of a defense contractor. Won't go over so well with the DOD."

"Exactly—so keep it by the book. The wife is Mary Ann and she's one of the sweetest people I know. If she's right, I want to do right by her."

"Now you're scaring me. Compassion? Where's the cutthroat legal shark who's always out for blood?"

"Not that compassionate. There's more to the story. The woman Tom is seeing—allegedly—works for him. Mary Ann is convinced there is more to it than an affair. She's scared she wants the business, too."

"Any proof?"

"That's where you come in. Need pictures, recordings, any other evidence you might come across, plus do a background on the girlfriend, mistress, whoever she is."

"Do you have her name?"

"Mary Ann will fill you in." He stood. "Be right back."

"She's here?" I said.

"In my office. Johnny, she's good people."

"I'll do my best."

I helped myself to another splash of Jim's expensive single barrel bourbon and watched the cranes load containers on the cargo ships in the harbor. A few minutes went by when the door opened and Jim entered with Mary Ann Bellamy. A petite woman with dark hair pulled back from a friendly, round face, large blue eyes, and a wide smile. I figured her to be around fifty. She wore a simple black dress that came to her knees, and low-heeled black pumps, as if she dressed for a funeral.

We went through introductions and pleasantries, and then Jim excused himself. We sat across the corner of the table from each other.

"Jim explained to me what you will do. Part of me is embarrassed and part of me is furious," she said. "We built a life together and I trusted him. Never thought of not trusting him. Now I sit here with a private detective, wanting my husband followed."

She had a hard time with the words and her eyes kept going to the floor. I detected the hurt in her voice and she kept her purse in her lap and flipped the handle back and forth as she talked. She sipped at her water, did everything she could to hold back tears.

I opened my notebook. "Mrs. Bellamy, none of this is pleasant, but it happens. I have worked many cases where—"

"It happens?" Her eyes now locked on to mine.

"What I mean is, these cases are more common than you think. I've seen all types—"

"Mr. Delarosa, this might be another job for you, but it doesn't happen to me. Us."

I let a moment slide by while I did my best to formulate an intelligent response. "I apologize. I'm sure you are hurting, but my experience in these situations, whatever your husband is doing, if he's doing anything, is—and I don't mean to sound cliché—call it a mid-life crisis, call it dealing with growing older and the fear of losing our youth...but, it happens. Wives hire me to follow husbands, and husbands hire me to follow wives. I'm sorry it happened to you."

"So, I'm just another victim?" She sipped the water again.

Could I dig a deeper hole for myself? "Why don't we first get the facts? I assure you, I work with the utmost discretion. Nobody will know anything about this but me, you, and Jim."

Her eye caught something through the glass in the outer hallway, and it caused her to glance out a second time.

"Oh, God," she said. "I know that man." Two of Jim's associates, a man and a woman, were chatting in the hallway. She angled her body in the chair so her back was to the corridor. "Tom cannot find out I was here."

"I'll ask Jim if there is another office we can use."

"I want to leave," she said, with her head down, staring into her lap.

"Can you come to my office?" I asked.

"When?"

"This evening? Seven?"

"Yes." I gave her my business card and she stood. "Is it clear?" she asked.

I leaned back in my chair to get a view. "They're gone."

"Mr. Delarosa, it's not a mid-life crisis. I'll explain later." She hung her purse on her shoulder, opened the glass door, and disappeared into the corridor. I poured a shot-worth more of bourbon.

The attractive and wealthy Mary Ann Bellamy was scared, nervous, and embarrassed. My curiosity, as they say, was aroused.

4

Mary Ann Bellamy arrived right on time at seven. I spotted her in front of McNally's, checking my business card with the address on the building. She finally ventured inside and stopped at the bar. Mike pointed her to the back and my office/booth. I met her half-way. She had changed from the black dress from this afternoon and now wore a simple button-down cream-colored blouse, blue jeans, and flat slip-ons. Her hair was in more of pony tail and the casual outfit took off ten years. The jeans flattered her; she had managed to hang on to a decent shape at fifty. My guess was a gym membership, personal trainer, tennis, yoga—the benefits of affluence.

"I was looking for an office building."

"It confuses folks." I led her to my booth. "Never saw much use for an actual office. Most of my work is referrals. Plus, I have a condo upstairs where I keep files and such. Can I get you anything?"

Her eyes scanned the bar. "I don't think. I'm not much of a drinker."

She sat and I slid in opposite her. "Mrs. Bellamy, I realize this is not what you were expecting, but you hired me for my experience, not because I have a fancy office."

She nodded. "Jim said you're the best at what you do. I trust his opinion."

Mike came over and I introduced them. He sat next to her and immediately picked up her trepidation. He was an imposing presence and no doubt her sitting in a blue-collar beer joint with two ex-cops was not her comfort zone. "Mrs. Bellamy, Johnny filled me in a bit and I want you to know we are here to help you."

"Jim didn't give me any background. Only that you will find what I...what I need to find out." She blushed.

"We were partners, PCPD, for many years. I retired, opened this place and a few years later, he bought in. He does the detective work and he's the best in the biz. Trust me when I say you're in good hands."

The tall, barrel-chested, redheaded Irishman could be charming and comforting when he needed to be. He took one of her dainty, well-manicured hands into one of his large, meaty paws. "Whatever information Johnny uncovers for you, good or bad, life has a way of working itself out."

"I hope," she said.

He let go of her hand and stood. "Drink?"

"Yes, that would be nice after all. Do you have a Riesling? Mosel Valley? Or the Willamette Valley from Oregon?"

Impressive for not much of a drinker.

Mike cocked his head. "I'll be right back."

Mary Ann turned to me and smiled. "You were both police officers?"

"Yes, twenty years, and we've seen it all. So relax and speak freely, nothing to be embarrassed about. Tell me what happened. When did you first suspect?"

"Six months ago. He became different. Detached. Irritable. I thought it was work pressures. They bid on a new contract and were waiting for the approval. Always a stressful time because his entire business relies on the government contracts. If they go away, then the company goes away."

Mike came back with drinks. "Best I could do was Napa Valley." He handed her the white wine and set my usual two fingers of bourbon in front of me.

"Perfect. Thank you," she said. Mike left and she sipped the wine and savored it for a moment before swallowing. "I needed that."

"Some liquid courage never hurts."

The drinks broke the ice and she relaxed and gave me the story. She explained how the company did win the approvals and contracts were signed between BST and the Department of Defense. The new cash infusion improved Tom's mood but their home life also changed. The new contract required Tom to travel to NASA's space flight laboratories in Maryland and to visit manufacturers in a few undisclosed locations. "At least undisclosed to me," she added. "Tom had brought on a new employee, a woman who was some sort of expert in aerospace technologies. A real rocket scientist. The next thing I knew, she was traveling with him to his meetings. Then working much later than he ever had. When I confronted him, he always said the new contract required much more of his time but it would pay off."

"The woman's name?"

She took another sip of her wine. "Keira. Keira Kaine."

"Did you ever meet her?"

"Yes, many times. At first I thought she was a perfect fit for the company. He needed help with research and design, and she came along with all these credentials. Then it became all Keira, all the time. She was all Tom talked about. Keira is amazing. Keira's ideas are incredible. Keira was the smartest decision he ever made. Keira could charm the pants off a priest. Of course, she's tall, blonde, beautiful, and confident."

"Do you know anything about her background?"

"Not much. They met at a conference. She came from the West Coast, I think. He once told me she worked for a competitor. They are together all the time. She goes with him on the NASA trips and to the other labs."

"Are you sure this is what you want me to do? I've had clients who were hell-bent on me finding out everything I could about what the spouse was doing, then when I present the evidence, they get angry with me when I put reality in front of them. Do you understand?"

"I need the truth." She finished her wine.

"Includes photographs and recordings, if possible."

She nodded. "I need to know if he is content in destroying our life for...for that woman."

"Today you mentioned this is not a mid-life crisis. What did you mean?"

"I'm worried about the company. Not too long ago, out of the blue, he mentions giving her part ownership. Said she deserves it. I realize I sound like a jealous wife, but he's worked too hard to give up any ownership. Anyhow, we ended up in a screaming match and he stormed out. Didn't come home for three days. Said he checked in to a hotel because he needed time. He was with her." She held up her wine glass. "Any chance?"

I went to the bar and came back with the bottle and refilled her glass. "Mrs. Bellamy—"

"Mary Ann. Please."

"And you call me Johnny." We touched glasses to seal the first-name basis. "Let me go to work. None of this is pleasant, but let's first find the truth."

"I feel so hurt and embarrassed. We had such a strong marriage. I can't believe it."

We continued with the conversation and the wine allowed her to relax and open up with me a bit. She told me about their son, Adam, who was in his first year of med school at the University of North Carolina. Pre-med and he was their pride. She was afraid to think how this divorce—if it happened—would affect him and the relationship with his father. I was never helpful with words of comfort and consolation, so I leaned back to what Mike said. "Life has a way of working itself out."

Katie came in and I introduced them and explained how she handled the background research for me. Katie's upbeat personality kicked in and turned the conversation friendly. Mary Ann relaxed and even laughed at Katie and her quirky goofiness. Katie complimented her jewelry and clothes; they covered fashion, shopping, vacations, manicures, spas and hair salons. I sat back and observed the easy conversation between two women, one a mother and one a daughter, and wondered whether Mary Ann looked at Katie like the daughter she never had. Or, the perfect mate for her son?

Katie grabbed my shoulder. "This man—the greatest boss ever—promised me time off for my vacation. I leave for San Juan in less than a week."

"You'll love San Juan," said Mary Ann. "Just beautiful. Tom and I went there three years ago and..." Realization of the moment stopped her. "Well, you'll love it."

We wrapped up the meeting with Katie jotting down some pertinent information vital to us investigating Keira and keeping an eye on Tom. Addresses, birthdates, upcoming business trips, favorite restaurants, and any other information Mary Ann could provide on Keira, which wasn't much.

I walked Mary Ann to her white Lexus SUV and she surprised me with a warm hug that she held a moment longer than I expected.

"Thank you, Johnny. You made me comfortable and I appreciate it."

"Do yourself a favor and take a deep breath. I'll be in touch in a week or so, and you can go from there. In the meantime, stick to your normal routine. Don't do anything out of the ordinary."

"I understand. Thanks." She smiled and climbed in her car.

Inside, Mike stood with his arms crossed.

"Something on your mind?" I went behind the bar and poured a second drink.

"You're taking a cheating spouse job? Pretty lady and all, but a bit on the routine and boring side."

"Decent fee on this one. I spent my money buying the beach cottage, now I need cash for renovations."

"Cyber-security is where the money is."

"Cyber-security? I can't even turn on my computer."

"That's why you have me." Katie had come over to the bar and poured herself a draft and parked herself on a stool. "Cool lady. Too bad she married a scumbag."

"Don't judge. We need facts."

"Came off like a rich, lonely wife with nothing to do but snuggle up to a bottle of white wine every afternoon. Husband comes home, nothing happens in the bedroom, so he goes elsewhere. We've seen it a million times," said Mike, with his jaded wisdom. "Johnny, my boy, the door to her bedroom will be wide open for you to slide right in. And if you don't, I will."

"Sexist." Katie punched Mike in the arm.

"Whatever, little girl. You'll see." She punched him again. "I have work to do."

He went to the kitchen and I finished off my drink. "First thing tomorrow, start full backgrounds on the Bellamys, the company, and Ms. Kaine."

"I will, but we need to wrap this one up fast. My vacation—"

"—your vacation starts in four days. Believe me, I know."

5

The North Shore community is an upscale confluence of mini-mansions on two-acre lots, with each house backing to a fairway of the North Shore Country Club, a thirty-six hole layout with swim and tennis, spa, and a clubhouse with a pro shop, two lounges, and a four-star restaurant. Affluent living at its finest, fifteen quick miles from the center of downtown Port City. It was the land of perfectly manicured lawns, backyard pools, and three-car garages stocked with expensive cars. Private schools are not a luxury; they are the norm.

Tom and Mary Ann Bellamy lived on Lark Way, a winding, tree-lined road that ran parallel between the fourteenth and fifteenth holes. The Bellamys' house backed to the fourteenth fairway; the homes on the opposite side of the street bordered the fifteenth. Fifty yards from the Bellamy house, I found a narrow dirt access path used by the golf course maintenance crew that snaked through the trees from the street to the course. Backing in, it gave me a concealed observation point. I drove my BMW Z4. I usually employed my Buick LeSabre for surveillance, but in this neighborhood, the LeSabre would be more conspicuous than the Z4. The kink in my plan would be if the grounds crew needed to access the road. It was six thirty a.m. and the goal was to record Tom's morning routine, snap a few pictures of his car, follow him to his office, and possibly catch a morning Keira Kaine rendezvous.

I lowered my window and the cool morning air brought in the scent of pine and freshly cut grass. I clicked a 300mm lens on my Nikon and didn't have to wait long. At seven fifteen, the left door of the Bellamy's three-car garage went up and I brought the camera to my eye. Mary Ann's white Lexus SUV backed out, just as a man came from the front door of the house and stood in the middle of the driveway with his hands parked on his hips. The car came halfway out of the garage and stopped. The man, I presumed Tom Bellamy, and the car, were in a standoff. After a minute, the driver's door opened and she emerged, wearing a white bathrobe, and confronted him. I heard voices but could not decipher any words. Arms flailed and fingers pointed and several volleys went back and forth before Mary Ann got back into her car and pulled into the garage. Tom charged in and a door slammed.

At seven thirty, a light-blue hatchback stopped in front of the house. "Honey Bee Maid Service," was stenciled on the side and the back of the car, along with a Port City phone number. A short, round, Hispanic woman hopped out. She raised the back hatch and removed a cart that she loaded with a broom, cleaning supplies, and a vacuum. I photographed the woman and the phone number. She pulled her cart to the door and rang the bell. A moment later, the door opened and she entered. Five minutes after that, the center garage door went up and a forest-green Range Rover SUV backed down to Lark Way, then straightened and shot past me. As I set my car in gear, I noticed Mary Ann standing in the driveway with her arms crossed over her chest. She watched him drive off and then turned and went back inside. I wondered whether she saw me in the trees, but after what I witnessed, I figured she had to be preoccupied with the morning argument to see anything.

I caught up with Bellamy at a traffic light as he made the left on North Shore Boulevard. I fell in fifty yards behind him. We went two miles when he turned in to a shopping center and parked at a coffee shop. I found a spot thirty yards from the store with a direct sight line. He went in and came out with a coffee cup and a newspaper in hand and took a seat at an outdoor table.

Twenty minutes went by and the shop bustled with patrons but Tom stayed at this table which I took as unusual. Most executives at his level, at least from my observations over the years, would grab breakfast and head into the office. He had time to leisurely sip his coffee and read the paper? My instincts, my gut, my sixth sense, got me through twenty years on the police force and six as a private investigator, and now it told me to hold tight.

A black Mercedes SL 450 pulled in and stopped beside the Range Rover. A tall, lithe blonde got out and walked to the table. Mid-thirties, I decided. She wore a dark-blue business suit, a white blouse, and flat shoes. She had to be five ten and if I was to guess her profession, it would be a fashion model—definitely not a rocket scientist. She sat across from Tom. I used the camera to get in close and clicked off a few shots. Beautiful, with an angular face, high cheek bones, a pixie-like haircut and everything screamed of money and class. The clothes, the car, the hairstyle; the way she sat upright in the chair with her hands folded in the lap. Tom did most of the talking and she nodded, smiled. He got up and went into the shop and she picked up the newspaper. I photographed her license plate and his.

I called Katie's cell and she answered after six rings. "You can't be serious?"

"Sorry. I'm sending you a couple of plate numbers. Tom Bellamy and I think, Keira Kaine. Run them first thing." Silence. "Katie?"

"Send them." She hung up.

Not a morning person.

Bellamy came back with a coffee for her and the conversation resumed. This time, her body language changed, the smile receded, her brow furrowed, and her arms crossed over her chest. Did he tell her about the argument with his wife? They talked for five more minutes and then departed in their respective vehicles.

I trailed behind both cars as they made the commute to Bellamy Space Technologies. Tucked away at the far end of the business park, it was a rectangular, one-level white building, surrounded by a ten-foot-high, black-iron fence. The company name was not displayed anywhere on the building, and the only windows in the entire structure were in the lobby. Four satellite dishes were mounted on the roof. Their cars stopped at a security gate to show identification, and then were waved through.

I drove past a quarter of a mile, made a U-turn, and came back and pulled to the roadside one hundred yards from the entrance and made quick work of snapping photos of the building. Last thing I needed was security to spot me taking pictures. I would have every three-letter government agency knocking on my door within minutes. The only way in was through the front gate, which made for tough surveillance.

Project Thomas Bellamy was underway. His wife hired me to prove his affair with Keira Kaine. So far, it appeared he wouldn't disappoint.

6

"Now what?"

"Chicken salad on a croissant with lettuce and tomato." Katie plopped into the booth opposite me. "Try it."

"It looks good, but I'm not so sure about our customers." I took a bite. "Delicious—but..."

"What? We need to keep reinventing ourselves if we want to compete in the restaurant business."

"How about we ease into this new menu thing after your vacation?"

"Fair enough—but this lunch menu is going to be killer. Then we work on the wine list."

"Wine list? What about Bellamy?"

I finished the sandwich while she retrieved her laptop. She sat beside me in my booth and opened the computer to a file she created. "Not much to talk about. He started the company fifteen years ago. A government contractor from what I can determine. There's a website." She turned the laptop to me. "It's only information about company leadership and the organizational history."

"They won't have contract details on the site," I said. We went through the web pages, and Katie was right. It featured bios of the senior executives: Thomas "Tom" Bellamy was President, Founder and CEO. Keira Kaine was Senior Vice President for Special Projects. *I wondered whether she's making Bellamy her special project.*

The site referenced advancements made in aerospace technologies and a trade journal article lauded BST and their groundbreaking work with GPS navigation and its applications to orbital satellites. A second story profiled Tom Bellamy and an award he received from NASA for his achievements with space-based solar power. *Whatever that is?*

"What else?"

"Nothing. All the articles I found were positive. All business. No juicy scandals or anything."

"What about Keira Kaine?"

"Well, interestingly, nothing. A Port City address. I can't find any history on her. I did credit and criminal and nothing."

"Nothing on her credit report?"

"One credit card and one car loan. Both with perfect payments. Both have the Port City address."

"No school loans?"

She shrugged. "I wish that was me." She flipped to another website. "Now, Bellamy, he's a player in his industry. A bunch of articles in trade journals about some space energy thing he discovered. Awards from NASA, a community award from a kid's charity." She clicked on a picture and it filled the screen. "Handsome guy. Self-made and all that."

"Yep, that's him."

"Mister Perfect got himself a girlfriend, huh?"

"Appears that way."

"Sleazebag."

"If it wasn't for cheating sleazebags, I'd be behind the bar serving drinks and you would be bored to death in some cubicle. What about Mary Ann Bellamy?"

"Not much. One article about a golf tournament-charity event where she was the chairperson. Nothing else. They have one son, Adam. Credit reports are excellent, mortgage, one car loan, four credit cards and a department store card. Looks all chummy on paper. This divorce will be major drama with the country club crowd."

"Any social media accounts?"

"No, none. Kind of weird. Nothing for Keira Kaine, either."

I slid out of the booth. "Keep digging. Mike is closing tonight. I'll be up in the condo."

"Don't forget, I'm leaving early. I need to shop. Can't expect me to go to San Juan without a new wardrobe."

"Wouldn't think of it."

***

The research continued at my kitchen table. I spent another two hours learning what I could about BST and government contracts. Not that the work BST does was integral to my investigation of Bellamy and his employee, but it was interesting that Katie found nothing on Keira Kaine. Nothing but a credit card and a car loan. *No school loans, not even a traffic ticket?* Everyone has a past, no matter how much we want to keep it hidden. Her past was too clean.

Employees of defense contractors must pass a background investigation that includes criminal, financial, and personal examinations to get their top-secret government clearance. If I was the investigator doing the background work for Keira Kaine's clearance, I would question the lack of a history on her. All I found was a previous address from San Francisco and a small mention of her name in an article from a Stanford University campus newspaper. It was as if she did not exist before coming to Bellamy Space.

I closed the computer, turned a jazz station up loud on my radio, made myself a quick cheese omelet, and grabbed a bottle of a Napa merlot and went to my balcony. The warm summer day had given way to a cool evening. I ate the omelet, filled the wine glass a second time, and stretched out on my lounge chair and watched the sinking sun provide a dramatic, swirling pastel backdrop to the Port City skyline.

My chirping cell phone shook me from a sound sleep. I answered and a woman on the other end identified herself as one Brynne Middleton, and said she was a friend of Mary Ann Bellamy.

"Mary Ann asked me to call you," she said. "She was in a car accident and is at St. Helen's."

"Is she okay?" I sat up and shook the fog from my head.

"She's banged up a bit, but the doctor said she'll be fine. She asked if you could come to the hospital."

"Who are you again?"

"Brynne. I'm her friend. She's in the emergency room."

"I'll be right there."

"Mr. Delarosa?"

"Yes?"

"She asked if you could be discreet. Said you would know."

"Of course."

I ended the call and checked the time. Eleven thirty.

7

St. Helen of the Cross Hospital was owned and operated by the Carmelite Sisters of Ireland and is the hospital of choice in Port City. Compared to City General, it was the Mayo Clinic. However, the emergency room at midnight was no different from any other emergency room: a waiting room crowded with the sick, injured, derelicts, junkies, crying babies, toddlers on the loose, tired mothers, a television blaring out a mindless talk show, a two-hour wait time, an empty vending machine, and a volunteer at the reception desk who can only tell you to take a seat.

I made my way through the battlefield of patients and past the useless volunteer and found a nurse who told me Mary Ann was admitted.

"Try the third floor," she said as she disappeared into the maze of the exam rooms.

The elevator dumped me out at the third floor nurse's station, where I inquired about Mary Ann. The nurse at the desk said without looking up, "Room 331. Turn left, on your right."

I made the left and caught the attention of a uniformed cop partway down the hall. "Delarosa." He approached with a hand extended. "Remember me? Jack Bridges."

"Yeah, Jack. Been awhile. How are you?"

"Sergeant now."

"Good for you. What's happened here?"

He nodded toward a small snack machine alcove, where we huddled. "Mary Ann Bellamy. She a client?"

"Yes. She okay?"

"She's lucky. Car accident on Spring Falls Road. She ended up halfway down the embankment toward the creek. Saved by a tree."

"Injuries?"

"Bruised ribs and a cut on her head. Husband is in there now with her friend. But, I got the impression the husband isn't aware she hired you. The friend told me she contacted you."

"Your impression is correct. Why are you here?"

"Said she was forced off the road."

"And...?"

"Something happened. She went through a guardrail but it doesn't add up. Too many skid marks for one car."

"Road rage?"

"Could be. She claims a van came up behind her and pushed her. What's the story?"

I shrugged. "Hired me yesterday. Suspects the husband of cheating. Alcohol?"

"Negative. Did a blood test here."

"Where was she coming from?"

"The friend's house. Spring Falls."

A woman came out of Mary Ann's room. She was a slim brunette, medium height, wore gray leggings, a black warm-up jacket, and had a short wedge haircut. She leaned against the wall and went to work texting on her phone.

"That's the friend," Bridges said.

"I could use a friend like that."

"No kidding. Hey, I'm done for the night."

I handed him a business card. "Mind sending me the accident location? I want to take a look."

"No problem. I can meet you there tomorrow morning if you want. Ten?"

"Perfect. Appreciate that."

"One thing, though. A tall blonde came in with the husband. She's in the waiting room." He pointed down the hallway.

"No kidding?"

"Hot, too. She the girlfriend?"

"Could be."

"Just when you thought you'd seen it all." He elbowed me. "Hey, I was in your place a few weeks back. Talked to Mike."

"Yeah? Hope he took care of you."

"He did. Cool place you guys have."

"Thanks. See you in the morning." We shook hands and Bridges left. I approached the friend. "Are you Brynne? I'm Delarosa."

"Oh, hi." She stuck the phone in her pocket. "Can we talk somewhere?" I nodded to the alcove and we went there. "She wants to talk to you but Tom is in there now."

"What happened?" She had lovely, light-brown eyes and I figured her around Mary Ann's age. Closing in on fifty or so.

"Somebody tried to kill her."

"Kill her?"

"Followed her, and then pushed her car through a guardrail. He did it. He wants her out of the way."

"You're talking about her husband?"

"Yeah, the jerk." Her eyes turned to daggers. "He actually brought the bitch with him here tonight. Can you believe that?"

"His girlfriend?"

"Yep."

"Does Mary Ann know she's here?"

"No. I didn't have the heart to tell her."

"Don't. I don't want the...other woman...to know I'm here, either."

"Oh, yeah. Right. I understand." Her phone beeped and she checked it. "It's her son. Let me answer him back."

"Sure." She typed away and a moment later, Bellamy came out of the room. I ducked back into the alcove. Brynne stopped typing and from my angle, I watched her stare at Tom as he collected a tall blonde—presumably, Keira Kaine—from the waiting room and disappear around a corner. If Brynne's eyes were lasers, she would have disintegrated the pair on the spot.

She turned back to me. "The bitch is putting it right in Mary Ann's face. I can't stand by much longer without confronting him."

"My advice, hold off for now. Can we go in?"

Brynne led me into Mary Ann's room. She was in the bed, her head bandaged, and her red eyes told me she had been crying. "Johnny. You came."

"Of course. How are you?"

Brynne handed her a tissue and she dried her eyes. "I have two bruised ribs and a cut up here." She tapped the bandage on her head. "Keeping me overnight to look for signs of a concussion. I'll be fine. Physically."

"That is most important," I said.

"He did it. No doubt in my mind."

"Let's take one thing at a time. What happened?"

She explained a white van came up close behind her car. She went faster but the van stayed on her tail and when she got to the big left turn on Spring Falls Road, the van pushed her car through the railing.

"All I thought about...I would never see Adam again." The tears spilled and Brynne got more tissues.

"We'll find out who did this. I talked to the police officer and we're going back to the accident site in the morning."

"She's behind this. I'm positive."

"Mary Ann, you're upset. I understand..."

"You don't understand. I will not go home. I no longer feel safe." Her face blushed, her eyes welled-up again.

Brynne gave her a sip of water. "She's coming home with me."

"You tell your husband you're going to Brynne's?" I asked.

She shook her head. "We argued this morning. I confronted him about Keira and the late nights. He denied everything."

"He came here tonight and hardly acted concerned. Like this was a bother. He is such a walking boner," Brynne added gracefully.

"Rest. Call me tomorrow once you're settled." I reached out and she squeezed my hand.

"Johnny, thank you again. Told you it wasn't going to be your usual case." She smiled and I smiled back.

"You work on healing. I'll work on everything else." I let go of her hand and motioned for Brynne to follow me to the hallway. "You taking her to your place?"

"I'm not letting her out of my sight."

"You think her husband is capable of this?"

"Yes. Trust me."

I gave her my card and we traded contact information. "She's going to need someone to lean on. I'm glad you're here."

"She was a good friend to me during my divorce. She does not deserve this. I won't rest until the bastard is strung up by his balls." Her dagger eyes locked on me as if I were going to pay for the sins of every cheating husband.

"Well, proper investigation first. I'll call you tomorrow."

"Fine." She went back into the room.

I made my way out of the hospital, thinking Bellamy better ante up a generous divorce settlement before the divorced wives club dragged him to the woods.

8

Spring Falls Road connects the fashionable Spring Falls community with the North Shore neighborhood. Midway along the ten-mile stretch, the road makes a wide, sweeping left turn as it parallels Spring Falls Creek. A police cruiser, with the red and blues flashing, sat on the shoulder, parked behind two other PCPD crime scene vehicles. I pulled behind the cruiser. An accident investigation team had one lane blocked and were taking photographs and measuring skid marks.

Bridges met me at my car. "Delarosa."

"Sergeant. What's the thinking?"

"Let me show you."

I followed him to a mangled portion of the guardrail that failed to do its job. We stood at the top of an embankment that dropped a good two hundred feet down to the creek. "She was either speeding or had help for this much damage to the rail."

"Consensus is she had help. Definitely forced off the road." He pointed to a massive oak halfway down. "Lucky for her. If it wasn't for the tree, she would have been in the water."

"Damn. Where's the closest traffic camera?"

"A mile back toward Spring Falls. She first noticed the van right after leaving the friend's place. We're pulling the video now."

I glanced back at the road, the turn, and the angle of the approach to the guardrail. "If you were going to force someone off the road, this would be the spot to do it. No place to go but down. Yeah, this was deliberate."

"I agree. I'll call you if the video comes back with anything. With any luck, we'll get a hit on the van."

"Bridges, I appreciate you allowing me a look out here."

"Hey, you're still one of us."

We shook hands and I got back in my car and turned toward town. My client was forced off the road. *Why?* To kill her? Who gains? The husband, the mistress? Why not divorce her, pay her off, and shove her out of the way so he and Blondie can live happily ever after? Instead, he risks a murder rap? Doesn't make sense. Bellamy brought his employee/girlfriend with him to the hospital when visiting his wife. An arrogant bastard? Yes. A murderer? No. Mary Ann had it right: this was not a typical case and I had to admit, I was now intrigued, and bothered, at the same time. In my short time knowing the lovely Mrs. Bellamy, I liked her and I did not like seeing her hurt, either emotionally or physically.

Nevertheless, someone pushed her off the road. *Who and why?*

***

Katie was behind the bar when I got back to McNally's. The lunch crowd began to file in and I told her to join me at my booth when she had a second.

Mike lumbered over with two draft beers and slid into the booth. "So?"

"Somebody rammed her off the road, the husband is a world-class bastard, and my case ramped up to interesting."

"The cheating spouse case is now attempted murder?"

"Accident investigation was on the scene. Skid marks confirmed two vehicles. Forced her through the guardrail."

"She hurt?"

"Banged up. She'll be fine. Doesn't want to go home. Swears the girlfriend put it all in motion."

"What about you?"

"Way too early to make that call." I gulped down half my beer. "My favorite kind of case, though. Beautiful, pretentious people, lots of money, high drama, handsome retainer."

"Copy that."

"Here's the fun part. The husband brought the blonde to the hospital last night when he visited his wife."

"Damn. Huge balls there. The wife know?"

"No. Thought it best not to say anything."

"Wait—the husband is a defense contractor, right?" He sat back and crossed his arms over his chest. "He was the target. He was supposed to be in the car. Find out who has a beef with him." Mike downed his beer and got up. "You can thank me later."

Katie made her way to my booth and I filled in the details of what happened with our new client.

She slammed her palm on the table. "Shut up!"

"It's true."

"That nice Mrs. Bellamy got run off the road and the husband brings his girlfriend to the hospital with him?"

"Alleged girlfriend..."

"Whatever—the bastard." She got up from the booth. "Wow, I don't believe it." She paced around in a circle and then sat back down. "The dude wants her dead and out of the way. That scum. Now what do we do?"

"What she hired us to do. Secure evidence of their affair. Alleged affair."

"Figures, I'm going on vacation and we get a hot one."

"Cancel. Go later."

"No way. Mandy would kill me. What did the police say?"

"Evidence of two vehicles. Investigation ongoing, pulling all video footage in the area. You can go on vacation anytime. The Bellamys have me curious and I might need a second set of eyes on this one."

"Johnny, don't do this to me." She folded her arms on the table, put her head down and talked into the table. "We've been planning it for weeks. Sun, beach, frozen drinks, gorgeous half-naked men. I cannot cancel on Mandy at this late date. We leave in three days."

"All right. Just asking. Want to do some surveillance work this evening?"

The ice-blue eyes peeked up at me. "You have to ask?"

9

Mary Ann Bellamy called to tell me the doctor discharged her from St. Helen's and she was on her way to Brynne's home in Spring Falls. She gave me the address and asked if I would stop by. I made the half-hour trip and had no problem finding the Middleton house. A Tudor style mini-mansion, it sat at the end of a long tree-lined driveway. A royal-blue BMW 750 sparkled in front of a three-car garage.

I rang the bell and waited a few minutes. No answer. I pressed it again and instinctively touched my jacket to make sure my Beretta was in place. Another minute passed and I decided to check the back of the house. A green chain-link fence bordered at least a half-acre of a patio and pool area. The gate pushed open and it was as if I checked in to a posh Caribbean resort.

A roof provided shade for half the patio. Two tables with umbrellas and chairs sat in the sun. An outdoor wet bar, a brick pizza oven, and a stainless-steel gas grill were adjacent on a smaller flagstone area. Eight lounge chairs with red cushions, and each with a side table, were arranged around the Olympic-size pool. At the far end of the pool was a white guesthouse, and beyond that, through a group of tall arbor vitae trees, was a tennis court. Perfectly manicured plants, shrubbery, and flowers hid the fence around the entire perimeter. All I needed was Paco the cabana boy to come and take my drink order.

Mary Ann and the comely Brynne Middleton were nowhere in sight. Under the shade of the patio roof, two French doors opened into the house. I knocked again, and after a minute, I did pull my gun. I called Mary Ann's phone and it went to voice mail. I found Brynne's number and pressed call back. No answer.

The doors were unlocked. I was about to take a step into the house when I heard voices behind me. I turned and saw Mary Ann and Brynne coming out of the guesthouse. I holstered my gun and pulled the door closed. Brynne had her arm around Mary Ann as they chatted and slowly made their way to the patio. Mary Ann had on white shorts and a pink polo top; Brynne wore a short, yellow sundress that ended halfway down her long thighs and accentuated her shapely legs. They spotted me on the patio.

Mary Ann waved. "Johnny."

"Shouldn't you be resting?"

They greeted me with hugs.

"Don't worry, my nurse here is quite strict. I had to talk her into showing me the new guest-house."

"For guests I never have." Brynne pulled a lounge chair next to a table. Mary Ann winced as we gingerly helped her lie down. I took a seat at the table. "How about a drink? Ice tea for the patient, she's on meds, but I'm thinking gin and tonic for us?"

"I like the way you think."

"Be right back."

Brynne went into the house and I turned my chair to face Mary Ann. "How are you?"

"Frightened. I know they did it. Arranged it."

"Horrible what happened, but it's a big leap to make those accusations. We need to find evidence of any involvement."

"I don't need evidence. He wants me gone. That hurts more than my ribs. He treats me terrible. If I am out of the way, no alimony, and he gets Keira."

"Mary Ann, you've been with him a long time. You know him better than anybody does. Is he a person who is capable of murder? Reach deep in your soul and think. Was this something he could do?"

She got quiet for a moment. "No, he's not. He's a rocket scientist, for God's sake. A brainiac, a nerd. Suddenly, he's some passionate lover? She has him brainwashed. I'm convinced. I guess she does things to him that I never did." She closed her eyes.

"Does Tom know you are here?"

"No, but he'll figure I'm with Brynne. He called my phone six times today but I didn't answer."

Brynne came out with the drinks. We toasted to Mary Ann getting better and a new life, to which she responded she was content with the old life.

I tried to spin it positive. "Concentrate on healing those ribs. I'll do what I can so we hand Jim Rosswell a solid case."

"Johnny, physically, I'll be fine, but emotionally I'm not. I am scared. I need protection. I'm lucky to be here today. The divorce can come later. Somebody rammed me off the road last night. It was no accident. She had me followed and tried to kill me...."

Brynne chimed in. "She's right. There's no other explanation."

"There can be other explanations. Mistaken identity," I offered.

"We all know that is not true." Brynne sat back in her chair and crossed her legs, allowing the dress to slide high on her leg. She caught me looking but I moved on.

"Mary Ann, my advice is to stay here for now. Let me continue my investigation. If I find anything that suggests Tom or the woman is responsible for last night, we will bring in the police. Plus, they have their own investigation. I want you to trust me."

"I am trusting you. I realize we just met, but I feel safe with you on my side."

"Get better." I took a gulp of my drink. "Brynne, you make a great gin and tonic, thank you." I set the glass on the table and stood. I took Mary Ann's hand in mine. "I'll check on you tomorrow."

Brynne got up. "I'll walk you out."

We walked around the house to my car. "Beautiful home. You live here by yourself?"

"Yep. There was a Dr. Middleton. He had the largest cardiology practice in Port City. At one point, they performed ten heart catheterizations a day. Then one day he stuck his catheter where he shouldn't. Now he is a fifty-six-year-old man with a three-year-old son and a thirty-three-year-old wife who is thirty pounds overweight. And I have this and two daughters away at college."

"I'm sorry that happened to you."

"I'm over it. Sort of. You?"

She was fun and funny but I had a feeling she could be fierce. "Divorced. Long time. Being a cop and being married didn't work for us."

"I get it." She put her arms around me in a tight hug. "When this is over." She let go. "Stop by anytime."

I opened my car door and smiled. "Might take you up on that, Brynne. Meanwhile, stay inside, keep the doors locked, and answer your phone."

"Yes sir."

I backed out of her driveway, watching the yellow skirt flit up and down as she walked around the house.

Steer clear, Delarosa. Steer clear.

10

My handheld rangefinder indicated we were two hundred and fifty yards from the front entrance of Bellamy Space Technologies. We found a spot in an empty warehouse parking lot on the opposite side of the road. I drove my surveillance vehicle—my eleven-year-old nondescript, tan, Buick LeSabre—in an attempt to be somewhat inconspicuous. Katie was tired of me constantly teaching her she must learn to be invisible to be an effective private investigator, but if the subject knows you are watching, you will never see anything.

Katie snapped a 300mm telephoto lens on the Nikon and focused on the front gate. I used the binoculars and scanned the building's parking lot. I spotted Bellamy's green Range Rover and Keira's Mercedes.

It was our second hour of surveillance.

"I can't hold this camera like this forever."

"It's not heavy."

"Not for you. The lens is heavy."

I got out of the car and opened the trunk. In addition to my briefcase of gadgets, I kept an assortment of old clothes I used for the occasional disguise. I grabbed a sweatshirt and back in the car, we used it to fashion a soft cradle on the dashboard for the lens.

"Happy?"

"Much better."

Thirty minutes went by with no activity. It was after six in the afternoon and I hoped Bellamy was getting close to quitting time. Katie put the camera in her lap, reached in the back and pulled a bottle of water from our cooler.

"That's your second bottle of water and you had a soda earlier."

"I'll be fine."

"We could be here for quite a while." I was not about to move this car after investing two hours. "You have to account for everything when on surveillance. Your surroundings. Will the cops spot you? Will someone else see you and call the cops? Somebody might think you are stalking someone. Are you close to a school? Last thing you need is someone thinking you are watching kids on a playground. And your food and drink consumption."

"I understand. I am a good student. I'll be fine."

Forty-five minutes passed.

Most of the employees had gone for the evening, leaving both Bellamy's car and Keira's car now clear in our sights. It would be impossible to miss them exiting the lot, except it was late in the day and we were now looking directly into the sinking sun. The light flares in the lens would block our vision and we would not pick them up until they reached the front gate, and I wanted to be ready and pull in position so I could fall in behind him as he left.

"C'mon Bellamy. Time to go home."

"Johnny?"

"Huh?"

"You don't want to hear this, but I need a bathroom."

I kept the binoculars to my eyes. "I'm going to pretend you didn't say anything."

She huffed and squirmed around on the seat. "I guess some things are easier for guys."

I nodded toward two small saplings in a grassy area near our spot. "Trees?"

"Funny. I wouldn't do that even if it was a gigantic bush."

"Too late. Bellamy and the blonde." I put the binoculars down and started the car. "You have them?"

"Yep. Bellamy is getting into his car and she is going to hers."

"Keep on him for now." I stopped the Buick at the edge of the lot. "As soon as he goes through the gate, I'll go."

The Range Rover passed through the security shack and turned away from us on the business park drive. I got lucky and pulled out without having to wait for traffic. We fell in fifty yards behind Bellamy.

"Did you take pictures?"

"What?"

"Pictures. Did you take any?"

"Of him pulling out?"

"Yes. The camera has time and date. Plus Wi-Fi. We can email ourselves the pictures and it establishes a timeline."

"I didn't..."

"Mark in your notebook he left work at six fifty-five." She made notes while we stopped at an intersection. The light changed, Bellamy turned, and we followed. I hung back and put two cars between us. A quarter of a mile later, he took the exit for the interstate. He punched the Range Rover and shot over to the far left lane. I stayed in the middle and a good ten car lengths behind. He would have to move right when it was time to get off, but a mile later, he passed the North Shore exit.

"He's not going home, is he?" Katie read his address from her notes.

"I hope not, for our sake. We need them to show up together somewhere. We take a few pics of them being cozy, and we put this case to bed. So to speak. Then we collect a fat payday and you go on your vacation."

"We need to get to somewhere fast. I can't hold it much longer."

Bellamy took the exit for downtown. "Hang in there. Keira lives in the city, right?"

Katie flipped a page in her notebook. "All we have is her car registration address. Ninth Avenue."

"Perfect. With any luck, we're going to Blondie's."

11

Bellamy did not go to Keira's home. He led us three blocks past Ninth Avenue to a neighborhood bar called, the Dark Side. He parked in an adjacent lot. We pulled to the curb and waited until he went in, then we drove in. From my spare clothes box in the trunk, I put on a pair of clear-lens, black-framed glasses, a ball cap, and an old jacket. I opened my attaché case, removed two portable GPS transmitters, and handed them to Katie.

"You know what to do?"

She nodded.

I took a silver ballpoint pen from my case and slipped it in my jacket pocket. "See you inside." Katie remained at the car with instructions and a full bladder.

The Dark Side was a narrow, rectangular space with no more than forty seats total. I took a seat at the bar that ran the length of one wall. The opposite wall had a row of two-seater high-tops. A few tables were in front and Bellamy had the corner table, thirty feet from me. A martini was on his table and he typed away on his cell phone.

Two middle-aged men, both in business suits, sat to my right with their attention focused on a baseball game on TV.

The bartender, a kid in his twenties, wearing blue jeans, a black Dark Side T-shirt, and a backward Phillies ball cap, slid me a coaster. "Bourbon, neat." He grabbed a bottle from the rail. "Hey, top shelf." He stopped, acknowledged my excellent taste in the great American distilled spirit with a nod, and then put the bottle back and reached high.

No sooner did he serve my bourbon, than Keira came through the door and sat at the table with Bellamy. They were behind me to my left. She was striking in a sleeveless green dress that worked perfect with the blonde hair. Bellamy called for another martini.

Katie burst through the door. "Ladies' room?" The bartender pointed to the back and she wasted no time. She turned the heads of the two gents down the bar as she blew past them.

The bartender delivered Keira's drink to their table.

I called him over when he returned. "Vodka tonic for the girl who just flew by." I cocked my head to the left. "Those two? Been in here before?" He sized me up for a second and I got the message. I pushed a twenty to him.

"Who are you?" I flashed my old police badge and hoped he did not have some deeply rooted disdain for authority. "Not sure." I slid him another twenty. "Don't know their names. The woman has been in here. Hard to forget her. The dude is familiar. She's been in here with other guys, too."

"Is that right?"

"Seemed all business, though. Comes in a few times a week. Sometimes by herself. Why, what did they do?"

I shrugged.

"They must've done something or you wouldn't be here. Let me use my expert bartender skill of analyzing people and dispensing advice." He looked past me and to their table. "My first guess is they are having an affair. Probably work together, but the body language is not right. Her arms are crossed in front of her. Defensive. He's been on his phone the entire time. There's tension; and if they are having a fling, it has now turned into an argument."

"I stopped trying to figure people out. I'm never right."

"I'm right, aren't I? About the affair part?" I sipped my bourbon to avoid a response. Katie came out of the restroom. "Here comes your blonde."

"Employee."

"Of course she is." He winked and walked away.

Katie took the seat to my right. "Oh my God. Barely made it."

"The cars?"

"Yep, both."

"The lovebirds are to my left. Angle yourself toward them a bit."

The bartender came back with her drink. "Thanks. Last thing I need is a drink but I need a drink," Katie said. Confusion on the bartender's face. He moved on.

I pulled the ballpoint pen from my jacket pocket. "Come closer. Snuggle in like we're lovebirds." Katie scooted her stool over and leaned into me. I showed her the pen. "This is a camera—"

"What?"

"Quiet. A camera. My angle is bad. Put it on your lap and point it toward their table. Click the top, and it takes a picture." I checked that the bartender was tending to the businessmen.

"No way—"

"Katie. Please. Point it in their direction and click."

She held the pen in her lap, angled it toward the table, and clicked. She leaned in and whispered in my ear. "Coolest job ever."

I whispered back. "Maintain your cover. Put the pen in your purse." She did, and then took a generous sip of her vodka.

The bartender came back. "You two okay?"

Katie smiled at him. "Yep." He went to Bellamy's table. "Selfie."

"What?"

"Let's take a selfie." She hopped off the stool and tugged at my sleeve. "C'mon, baby." She said it loud enough for all to hear, but I got it. She turned our backs toward Bellamy and Keira and held her cell phone camera high. She extended her arm and snapped away.

"I think you cut my head off. Try again."

She snapped a few more. "Okay, I got it." She planted a kiss on my cheek. "Thank you, baby."

The bartender wandered over as we settled back on the stools. "You want me to take your picture?"

"Nah, we're fine." Katie nudged me in the ribs. "Aren't we, honey?"

"Yes we are." I smiled into those magic blue eyes.

Voices came up from Bellamy's table. A chill went up my spine. *Did they make us? Did the bartender tip them off?* Katie turned. I yanked her arm. "Don't." They were arguing. I could only make out a few words but I heard Bellamy saying, "I can't believe you" and "Ruin a good thing."

The bartender stopped in front of us. "Trouble in paradise, huh?"

"Sounds like it," I said.

Chairs scraped on the floor. Katie peeked. "She's leaving." Keira was up and out.

Bellamy yelled, "Money's on the table."

"Thanks, buddy." The bartender waved as Bellamy went through the door. He turned to us. "You two want another?"

"We're done." I threw some bills on the bar. Katie finished off her drink.

She grabbed my arm. "I'm glad we're not like that couple."

"Me too, honey. Me too."

***

"The pen is a camera? So freakin' cool! You going all James Bond on me?"

"Concentrate on the laptop, please." We were in the car, tracking Bellamy and Keira's cars with the GPS trackers. Katie had stuck the trackers, encased in a magnetized housing, on their cars before coming into the bar.

"He is on the interstate...took the exit for North Shore so he's headed home. Keira is not anywhere close to Ninth Avenue."

"Let's try to catch up with her."

"Turn right at the next intersection. Should be Madison. She's on this street about a mile ahead of us. So how do we get the pictures out of the pen?"

"Mini-SD card inside. We'll pull them up on your laptop tomorrow morning."

"Cool. I want one. Once I dated a guy in college and I thought he was cheating on me with this skank cheerleader. If I had a camera pen, I could have—"

"Not now, please. Concentrate."

"Okay, okay. She turned right on Southland Boulevard." We turned on Southland but only went a block when the blinking cursor stopped. "Wait, she's making a U-turn." We moved to the side of the road, out of the traffic.

"Let's stay here for a second."

Katie swiveled the laptop to me. "She's coming this way." We waited and thirty seconds later her Mercedes went by, heading back to where we started. I pulled from the curb and swung around, keeping five or six car lengths between us. She made the turn back on Madison, passed the bar, and then turned on North Avenue, went four blocks to a row of modern, four-level townhomes on the left. A garage door opened on a home in the middle of the block and she pulled the Mercedes in. The door closed and we sat for a moment.

"She's mad, and needed a drive after the argument? Or, she went to find a girlfriend to talk to?"

"Don't speculate. We deal in facts."

"Did we get what we need?" Katie asked.

"We're hired to produce evidence of them having an affair. So far we have pictures of them having drinks in a bar." She flipped through the selfies on her phone, all deliberately aimed past us. She had three clear shots of Bellamy and Keira at their table. "Sharp thinking, though. It establishes them meeting after work. Adds to the case. Too bad we couldn't listen in on their argument."

"Thanks." She held her phone to me. "I love this one." It was a selfie of the two of us. "We are so cute."

Our cheeks were pressed together; we had wide smiles and looked as if we were meant to be. "You're cute. I look old—plus I'm wearing fake glasses."

"Exactly. By the way, you still have the glasses on."

12

A rap on the window of McNally's, which we ignored because someone knocking at ten in the morning was usually a homeless person looking for a handout, interrupted our session of self-congratulations. We had the mini-SD card was out of the camera pen, into an adapter, and into the laptop. We scrolled through the pictures and marveled at the quality of our furtive photography of Tom Bellamy and Keira Kaine.

"I'm def buying one of these pens. What else do you have? These gadgets are important for my career. I need the latest high-tech equipment."

"One thing at a time," I said.

A second knock got Katie to lean out of the booth for a view of the door. I pushed myself up for my own observation.

An older man in a business suit had his hands cupped around his face as he peered through the window.

"I'll go." Katie hopped out. She took yoga in the mornings and still wore her yoga pants and a tight T-shirt. Her tall, beach volleyball-player body defied any man not to stare. I admired the view as she went to the front and then was mad at myself for my inherent objectification of women. However, at age forty-eight, I doubt my faults are fixable.

She unlocked the door, talked to him for a minute, and led him back to the booth. I noticed him sneaking a peek at her backside as he followed her. I stood to meet him.

"This gentleman is here about Mrs. Bellamy."

I extended a hand. "Johnny Delarosa. How can I help you?"

"Mr. Delarosa. My name is George Ainsley and Mary Ann is my niece." He paused, glanced at Katie. "Can we talk here? I did not expect to find you in a bar."

"Yes, we can. I own the place and Katie is my assistant."

I offered him a seat and had Katie grab some coffee. I sat opposite him. He was thin, over six feet tall, and wore a black suit jacket that hung on him, gray dress pants that were an inch too short, a white shirt, and a wide, red tie held in place with a gold tie bar. He had to be around seventy and had thinning, silver hair pasted across his scalp.

He folded his hands on the table and looked me in the eye. "Mary Ann told me she hired you, but there is more to her situation. She is in grave danger. The car crash two nights ago was no accident. It was deliberate."

"Ainsley, right?" He nodded. "Why don't you start at the beginning?"

He hesitated. Almost scared to let the words out. "No doubt in my mind they want her dead. I have seen and heard things that make me afraid." He glanced at his wrist watch.

"Serious allegation. You want to explain?"

"I supported Mary Ann's decision to hire you and move forward with a divorce. Tom Bellamy has humiliated her beyond all reason."

Katie returned with coffee for the three of us. She sat beside me and opened her notebook. "Why are you here?"

"Keira Kaine. She's poison. They think I'm some old guy at a desk and ignore me. But, I'm not dead yet. The entire culture of the company changed when Tom hired her." The timbre of his voice went up, his face flushed, and beads of sweat appeared on his forehead. "He met her at a conference in San Francisco two years ago and the next thing you know, she is running R&D and our operations, with access to all company files."

"Mr. Ainsley, slow down. I understand you're upset, and you resent what she's doing to their marriage—"

"Damn right, I resent it. Not only their marriage, but what she's doing with the company." He pushed up his sleeve to look at his watch again. "You need to find out about her. Who she really is."

"Keira Kaine?"

"If that's her real name." Katie kicked me under the table. "I know I sound like a raving lunatic. The old man who's lost his mind."

"We are not saying anything."

"I want a background investigation done on her. I tried myself and found nothing." Katie was scribbling as fast as she could. "What's suspicious—she had a top-secret clearance when she came to work for us, but I can't verify any past employers. She claims she was a consultant."

Katie sat back in the booth. "You asked her about her past jobs?"

"Only in general conversation. I never questioned her about her background."

We all took a breath. I let Katie continue. "Do you get along with her? Are you in the same department?"

"Our relationship at work is cordial, at best. I was Tom's first employee when he formed the company. He and I worked together at another aerospace firm, and when he made the decision to open his own firm, he took me with him. I introduced him to Mary Ann. So, I am upset."

I made an attempt to make some sense of the conversation. "Mr. Ainsley, I understand your concern, but I'm not sure what we can do. Mary Ann hired us to help with her divorce."

"It's like she didn't exist before she met Tom. Something is not right. I'm worried about Tom, Mary Ann, and the company."

"I'm not sure—"

"I will hire you. We need to know who she is and what she wants. The money, your fee—it doesn't matter. She will destroy us." He checked his watch again.

"You keep checking the time."

"They are watching me. We are a government contractor and hold fiduciary responsibilities to our national security. If the DOD gets nervous about our senior executives, they can pull our contracts."

Was he veering toward conspiracy theory? "Who is watching you?"

"They are. Keira's people. You need access into our files. Use a hacker or something. I can't help you. They track everything. Even our keystrokes are recorded."

"What would we search for?"

"Anything that she's touched. Any file, any drawing, blueprint. Communication. Her emails, letters. What is your fee?" He pulled a checkbook from his jacket.

"Mr. Ainsley. We are not at that point. I need much more information before taking on something like this."

"I would be more comfortable if I had you on a retainer. So we develop the confidentiality of a client relationship." He glanced at his watch again. "How much. I'm out of time."

He began to write out a check. I put my hand on his and he stopped. "Mr. Ainsley. Sit back for a second." He considered us, and then leaned back in the booth. "Take a breath. I want to help, but we need more."

"I'm sorry. I'm not thinking straight. The accident and all. We need a safe location anyhow."

"Safe location?"

"Yes, at least for Mary Ann. Can you arrange that? There is much to discuss."

"Mr. Ainsley—"

"Please. The stakes are huge here. You can help us." Purple veins in his long, slender neck bulged out above his collar. I feared he was at the point of explosion. "Please."

I gave him a business card. "Call me this evening."

"I'll do that. I must go." He shook my hand and slid out of the booth. "Thank you both."

Katie got up. "I'll show you out."

He buttoned his jacket. "One thing though. Are you familiar with space-based solar power?"

"No."

"You will be. And one more thing? She's bad. Trust me." He acknowledged Katie and headed to the front door.

She leaned over to me. "Don't you dare move." She locked the door after Ainsley went out, and ran back to the booth. "Is he a nut job or do you believe him?"

"Not sure what to believe."

"So, now what?"

"We go see Mary Ann and ask about crazy Uncle George."

13

"Eccentric, yes. Crazy, no. You must to listen to him." Mary Ann sat forward in her chair, to emphasize her point. "He is one of the smartest people I ever met." She winced and sat back.

"He came off as worried. Paranoid," I said.

"He's been upset about Tom and Keira, and about the future of the company, for months now. If he came to you, then you need to take him seriously. He is a rational man, thinks and analyzes everything. He would not react to this emotionally."

Brynne put a bottle of Chardonnay and three glasses on her patio table. "Mary Ann is right. The guy is a rocket scientist, analytical, methodical; no doubt he's thought this through from ten different angles." She poured wine for Mary Ann, me, herself, and then turned to Katie.

"Would you like an ice tea, sweetie? Or a soda?"

"The wine is fine for me, too. Thank you," she said.

"Oh, sure." Brynne went for another glass while Katie shifted in seat. The heat from Katie's boiling blood almost toasted my skin. I was afraid she was going to blow. There were three felines around this table and I feared one of them—my assistant—was either going to be drowned in the pool or eaten alive. These two lost their husbands to younger women, so like an idiot, I brought a tall, blonde, twenty-four-year-old with me to the meeting. When I introduced Katie to Brynne as my assistant, the reaction was so cold the chill went to my spine. Brynne set a wine glass in front of Katie. Mary Ann had to pass Katie the bottle.

"He was emotional. All over the place. He claims there is no information on Keira prior to coming to work for your husband. Is that true?" I asked.

"Yes, but only from my speculation. When I asked Tom about her, he was always vague. Said she worked as a consultant in the aerospace industry and he thought she would be a perfect fit."

"Mr. Ainsley said Tom met her at a convention, and I'm sorry to rehash this, but I'm not sure what to believe with him."

"True, they met at a work conference, and whatever my uncle says, is the truth."

"I second that," said Brynne. "George Ainsley is the definition of integrity. If he is concerned about the company, and what the bitch is doing, she must be up to something."

Katie made a brave attempt. "He sounded like a conspiracy theory nut. Those people who say the government is always watching." Mary Ann and Brynne stared at her for even having the nerve to talk. "I'm just saying." She took a slug of her wine and went back to the notepad.

"He's not that," Mary Ann said. "Johnny, whatever he wants, please do it. If he's asking you, he has real reasons."

"You are my client and you hired me to find proof of their affair. That, I can do. He asked me to investigate Keira Kaine under his suspicion she is undermining Tom for control of the company. Is he representing BST in this arrangement, or is he mad at what's happening with you and Tom?"

"Both. He is dedicated to his career and to Tom, who was like the son he never had. My Uncle George never married. His work was his life and now he is distraught. He was so proud of Tom and their accomplishments and equally devastated when he found out about Tom and Keira."

"He's insistent your accident—"

"It wasn't an accident," Brynne reminded.

"Insisting it was not an accident is a heavy allegation. I caution that what he wants me to do could be a product of his imagination."

She held up her wrist wrapped in cast. "I did not imagine this."

"Mary Ann, I'm sorry." We all took a breath. Poured more wine into our glasses.

"Johnny, do what he says. Please. I trust him with my life. He might come off a little eccentric, but I tell you he is not."

I turned to Katie. "What was the space thing he mentioned?"

She flipped a few pages. "Space-based solar power."

"Yep. Tom's claim to fame."

"What is it?" I asked.

"They launch satellites into space with solar panels that absorb the sun's rays. Solar power. The problem was sending the electricity back to Earth. Tom figured out a way to transmit it efficiently. The ultimate in clean energy. He is the world's foremost expert in this technology."

"Translation: the country develops and implements the technology, Tom and Keira become billionaires, and Mary Ann is the lonely ex-wife with an alimony," Brynne said.

Mary Ann gave her a sideways look. "Thanks for the pleasant glimpse into my future."

"I'm just saying." Brynne aimed a stare at Katie. "I'll get another bottle of wine."

"None for us. We need to go. Mary Ann, I will work with George. I'm supposed to talk with him tonight."

"Whatever he tells you will be the truth. He only deals in absolutes. He's a scientist. No emotion ever."

"I understand. You're going to stay here for a while?"

"Yes, I am. Until this business solved. Please call me after you talk to him?"

"I will."

Katie and I got up from the table and said our good-byes. We made it around to the front of the house and to the driveway when she let loose. "What a bitch. Can you believe how they were toward me? I work for you. What about respect for me? Not my fault they couldn't keep their husbands. Brynne thinks she's some hot shit because of her hot body and a lot of money. Major fronting, if you ask me. Jealous old bag. I hope I never turn into one of them. No wonder the husband cheated. Guaranteed a frigid bitch in bed...probably laid there like a dead fish while he went at it. I bet she was blow job Brynne in college, and once she got married—nothing. No problem spending the husband's money, though, huh? You could have said something."

"I—" *Don't do it Delarosa. Let her vent. Keep your mouth shut.*

"You're not going to say anything? Fine. You approve of the way they treated me? Rich country club bitches."

We got in the car and she slammed her door. I kept my mouth shut.

Her rant continued for twenty miles.

14

"Tell me about the space-based energy program."

"Spaced-based solar power. The cleanest energy possible. We use satellites with solar collector panels to absorb the sunlight and then transmit the energy to receiving stations on Earth. Solar technology was developed at the beginning of the space program, but the original challenge remains how to safely send the electricity back to Earth at a feasible cost." George Ainsley switched into rocket scientist mode. "Prior to now, the electricity could only be sent to Earth via microwaves or lasers, but the receiving terminals had to be massive. Kilometers in size. Tom Bellamy perfected a cost-efficient method using microwaves to pinpoint the transmission to smaller receiving stations. Once this technology is financed and implemented, it will be revolutionary."

Katie jotted notes as fast as she could. We were huddled around cheeseburgers and fries at a small table in the back of Nancy's Diner, a favorite spot of mine, owned by Nancy Carlisle. Her husband, Bill, was a cop and they ran the diner while he was still on the job. Cancer snatched him away leaving Nancy the restaurant to operate on her own. The cops keep an eye on her, and she keeps an eye out for them. The table was in a back room off the kitchen and I used it for my sometimes clandestine meetings. It also doubled as a poker table for a weekly game for guys from Bill's old unit. Ainsley agreed to meet us here for a late evening meeting.

"Does that work?" Katie asked. "You can send electricity to Earth from space?"

"Of course."

"A laser fired from space to Earth is a bit on the sci-fi side, right? Wouldn't interference be a factor, let alone the security issues?" I asked.

"Mr. Delarosa, you hit on the problem that plagued the industry for decades. Laser technology is less expensive, but fraught with potential peril. Weaponization and blinding to name two."

"Blinding?"

"Yes, don't stare into the laser." He smiled, leaned back in his chair, and let loose with a full-throated laugh.

An inside joke for rocket scientists?

The economic benefit would be life changing for the scientists who were first on the scene with this technology, but it also meant the government, competitors, other nations, and terrorists would want their piece of the pie. The upside was enormous and with that much of a payday, maybe Ainsley's paranoia was real.

Nancy approached the table as if she read my mind. "You folks need anything?"

"Delicious as always, my dear." I handed her a few of the empty plates.

"Johnny, could I talk to you for a second?"

I followed her to the kitchen.

"There is a dark-colored sedan parked at the end of the side street. Two men, been idling there since you three came in. You expecting company?"

"No, but my friend might be. Thank you. I can always count on you."

"Hey, I learned to keep my eyes and ears open, and my mouth shut."

"You're the best."

I went back to the table.

"Even though I'll never pretend to understand all the science and technology, I do understand a lot of money is at stake. Does BST own this technology? What about the government?"

"BST signed a joint venture relationship with the Department of Defense for our satellite work. Tom developed the microwave technology outside the scope of that contract. We are free to go to the private sector with the program. Of course, the government will want to be involved; their hands are in all our pockets anyway."

"What do you want from me?"

"Find a way into our company and uncover what Keira is doing. I can't do anything from inside, but I'm hoping—and I know this is risky—you can come up with some tech guy, a hacker or someone...who can hack into our computers, search around, get into her files, email, anything."

"If she wants the company for herself, she is smart enough to not leave a paper trail."

"No doubt you are correct, but I need to do something."

"Mary Ann asked me to help, and she has utmost respect for you, but I wouldn't know where to find a hacker."

Katie popped up from her note taking. "I do."

Ainsley and I both turned to her. "What?" I asked.

"You do?" Ainsley said.

"Kid I went to high school with. Eric Eichenberg. Got sent to prison for hacking into the government. The Army or the Pentagon or something. We all thought he was just some gamer nerd, but he turned out to be this computer genius."

"Where is he now?"

"Far as I know, he's out and in Port City. I can find out easy enough."

Ainsley almost came across the table. "Do it. Find him. At least find out if this is possible."

"Hacking into your company or anyone else is illegal. We can talk to Katie's friend but if he has any sense, I hope he's using his talents for the benefit of mankind."

"Please. Allow me to meet with him, which is all I'm asking." He addressed Katie. "Miss, can you get me in touch with him? Set up a meeting and it will be out of your hands."

She checked to me.

"We can contact him, but I need to advise against this," I said.

"Please, arrange a meeting. I will pay you for your time."

I sat back and studied George Ainsley for a minute. I believed Mary Ann. He was confident and comfortable when talking about his work, but when he talked about Keira, he was out of his comfort zone, and his desire to hire a hacker and delve into Keira Kaine's background was way out of the scope of his life.

"Mr. Ainsley, you told me you thought you were being followed. Did you see anyone tonight?"

"No, but I have seen them before."

I took a burner phone from my jacket pocket. "Call me tomorrow. My number is programmed in. Only use the phone to contact me, and I will only contact you on that phone." He held it in his hand as if I empowered him with world secrets. "Where is your car?"

"On Arbor, one block down."

I went to the kitchen and came back wearing a cook's apron and one of those paper caps that keep hair from falling into the food. I took a pack of cigarettes and a lighter from my jacket pocket. "Give me thirty seconds then leave through the front, the way you came in. Walk to your car, do not glance around, and go straight home."

"I call you tomorrow?"

"Yes, twelve noon." I pointed to Katie. "You stay here."

I ducked out the back door and to the side street. It was not much more than an alley, room for the trash bins and two cars to pass. I lit a cigarette and leaned against the building, giving myself a view Arbor Avenue, which ran in front of the restaurant. Seconds later, I saw Ainsley on his way to his car. The sedan Nancy spotted pulled down the side street. I angled my face away as it passed, and then watched as it turned in Ainsley's direction.

Back inside, I took off the apron and cap. "Call your friend. We can use him to talk Ainsley out of his hacking idea."

"I'll try tonight. Where did you go?"

"Later. Let's go."

We went out through the front and I grabbed Katie's hand once we were on the sidewalk. "We are now a couple."

"Was he followed?"

"No talking." We rounded the corner to the side street and strolled like two lovebirds on a date. A car engine started. I pressed Katie against the side of the building and buried my face into her neck. "Is a car coming?"

"Whoa. Um, yes. What are we doing?"

"Do not talk, observe," I whispered. "Make it look real." She put her arms around me as the car passed. "How many in the car?"

"Two men in the front. I think it was a Taurus."

"That was the tail car. Ainsley was followed. They probably made us, too."

We stayed in our embrace for a moment then made our way to my LeSabre and got in.

"Damn. My heart's pounding," she said.

"Sorry to surprise you, but you were perfect. Cool under pressure."

"The only thing, you hit my go spot."

"Go spot?"

"Tickle spot on my neck. It gets me going. I got goose bumps clear down my legs."

"Sounds like a good thing to me."

15

Eric Eichenberg spent thirteen months of a thirty-six month sentence at Janesville Federal Penitentiary for hacking into the Pentagon and the United States Army's payroll system. He explained to prosecutors that his sole motivation was to prove the government's computer networks were vulnerable, and that if he could hack in, then we were wide open to any foreign country. The Army was impressed, but not amused.

He was seventeen years old and charged as an adult.

At Janesville, he taught an intro to computer class to other inmates and in return for his exemplary behavior, he was released early and placed on probation for three years.

Katie put a box of doughnuts on the table and made coffee.

"He is a computer genius. Unbelievable." I closed my laptop after reading through four newspaper accounts of how he hacked the government and was caught and convicted. We were in my condo. If this all went as planned, I wanted to keep Eichenberg out of sight. No sense of anyone getting eyes on him, especially if my plan screws sideways. I would hate to be responsible for him being sent back to Janesville.

It only took three phone calls for Katie to track him down and he agreed to meet us here at nine. The knock came at eight fifty-eight.

She opened the door to a short, skinny guy, dressed all in black: boots, jeans, Megadeath T-shirt, and leather jacket. He had black hair in an odd shag-mullet combination with a ponytail. His ears were covered in piercings and he wore a ring on each finger. He had computer bag over his shoulder.

"Oh my God, Katie Pitts. After all these years." He came in and threw a hug around her. His head came up to her chin.

"Hi, Eric. Thanks for coming. Meet Johnny Delarosa."

He came to me with his hand outstretched. "Dude, nice to meet you. Katie told me about your cool private eye biz. Said you're helping her get a PI license."

Katie's face turned fire engine red.

"We're working on it. Please, sit. Coffee?"

"Sure. Cream and sugar."

"Thanks for meeting us. I appreciate you coming." I served the coffee and we sat around the table.

He could not take his eyes off Katie. "I can't believe it. When you said it was you on the phone last night, I about stroked. My God, you are hot. You went to school in Florida, right?"

"Florida State."

He turned to me and lowered his voice. "I went away after high school too, sort of lost touch." He turned to Katie. "Old friends, catching up."

"Well, we weren't really friends—"

He aimed at me. "This is a cool place you got here. You own the bar, too? Dude, ex-cop, private eye, owns a bar, hot babe works for you—this is jammin'. Should be a TV show or something. Video game—dude, I could create it!"

He dumped sugar and milk in his coffee and it slopped over the cup as he stirred. I cocked an eyebrow at Katie. She passed him some napkins, which he ignored.

"So you need some help, huh? I'm all ears."

"Well, I have a client who—"

"Katie, you look damn fine, girl. I cannot believe you called. This is amazing. You locked into a boyfriend or anything?"

"Nope, no boyfriend or anything at the moment."

"What happened to your dude, Brad or Tad, or something? Had one of those rich kid names."

"Um, we broke up after high school. I heard he got some girl pregnant in college and is now married."

"Dude, wouldn't want that scene. Too bad for him. What about the hottie, Mandy? You still friends with her?"

"Still best friends."

"She was hot in high school. She's gotta be smokin' now. Unless she got fat. BFFs, huh? Doughnut?"

"Sure." She slid the box to him.

He grabbed a chocolate frosted and finished it off in two bites. He pulled his laptop computer out of the case. "So, private eye, what's going down?"

He saw us both staring at a bumper sticker he had pasted on the outside of his laptop:

YEAST INFECTION: IT'S CONTAGIOUS

"That's my band."

Katie set her coffee on the table and folded her arms in front of her. "You're in a band called Yeast Infection?"

"Yeah, I play bass. Righteous mash of grunge, punk, and heavy metal. Laying it down loud and nasty. Writing our own stuff, too. We have a gig downtown on Saturday. You should come."

"Um, I'm going on vacation. Maybe another time."

"Dude, what about you? Might not be your thing, but there will be some cool babes there. They always dig the older dudes."

Out of the corner of my eye, I caught Katie biting her lip. "Can we get down to business?"

"Dude, I'm all in."

I explained about Ainsley, and what he wanted, and that we needed a hacker who can do some deep digging.

"Whoa, I can't hack. I can search around for you, but they still monitor me. They say they don't, but..."

"I understand. No hacking. I promise. Just need to appease the client a bit."

"Your wish. When is this going down?"

"Available tonight? Here, eight o'clock, park around back."

"Right on, dude. Cloak-and-dagger. I'm down. Katie baby, I'll ding your celly when I'm here."

He closed the laptop, gave me a fist bump, Katie a hug, and grabbed a doughnut on his way out.

She locked the door behind him and came back to the table.

"Sorry about that. I didn't know what to expect. I haven't seen him for years."

"If he called me dude one more time, I was going to throw him off the balcony. He couldn't keep his eyes off you."

"Please."

"He wants a shot at your go spot."

"Funny." She threw a piece of doughnut at me. "Dude."

16

Katie went downstairs to the bar to prep for her shift and I opened my computer to the accounting program. I had a mountain of invoices to enter and pay.

My phone chirped and I answered. It was Mary Ann. "Johnny, we're being followed. You need to do something." Her voice was frantic.

"Where are you?"

"Brynne drove me to the doctor and the same car stayed behind us the entire time. When we came out, we saw it again. Now, we are almost back to Brynne's, and he's behind us."

"Describe it."

"Dark blue. I think a Chevy. I could see the thing on the front."

"How many men in the car?"

"Two."

"Tell Brynne to go straight home and park in her garage. Stay in the house. Is the car close enough for you to take a picture?"

"No."

"How far are you from the house?"

"We're close. A mile or so."

"Get in the house and make sure the doors are locked. I'm on my way."

"Johnny, hurry."

I closed the laptop, strapped on my shoulder holster with the Beretta, and grabbed my keys and phone. I stopped in the bar on the way out and told Katie about the call and that I was headed to Brynne's house.

Her skepticism leaped out. "You sure they're being followed?"

"I'm not sure of anything. Only what they told me."

"They just want you out there. Bring your swimsuit."

"You are not helping."

"Sorry."

"Check the locations of Tom and Keira's car. I'll ding your celly if anything is up."

She shooed me out with a bar rag.

I went through the kitchen to my garage in the alley and pulled out the Z4. If Mary Ann was followed, and if it was the same guys who tailed George Ainsley from Nancy's, I wanted to make sure I used a different car. No sense in making it easy for them.

As I turned in Brynne's driveway thirty minutes later, the front door opened. Brynne stuck out her head and waved me in.

"We were watching for you. Thank God." She threw a hug around me. "Come in."

She took me to a homey, dark wood-paneled den that had a brown leather sofa and a matching recliner. A flat-screen TV covered one wall, a book case covered another, and a wet bar was in a corner. Dr. Middleton sure did screw up.

Mary Ann sat on the sofa and I sat down beside her. She filled me in how they first spotted the car when they stopped for lattés on the way to her doctor.

"We are not safe here. They know I am here. It is not safe for me, and not for Brynne. Can you find us someplace to hide out?"

"Mary Ann, your safety is the priority, but there are other things to consider."

"Nothing else to consider. We were frightened. The same car going, and coming back. The same two men. One wore a baseball cap."

Brynne was at the bar and I hoped she was working up gin and tonics.

"Mary Ann, I can find someplace for you. Maybe a hotel and we can hire a security guard. But until I can figure this through, we can bring security here?"

"I don't want some rent-a-cops in my house or their car in my driveway. I'm sorry. We'll scare the neighbors." Brynne set three drinks on the coffee table. "Gin and tonics okay? Mary Ann, take it easy—remember your medication."

"Exactly what I need. Works wonders with my pain pills," she said.

We all took a healthy sip. I raised my glass. "Brynne, must be your specialty."

"I try."

"You can always go back to your house and we ask Jim to start a legal separation agreement and make Tom move out."

"I'm all for the separation. The argument we had the day he tried to kill me was the final blow. But, I am not going back to the house until he is out. In fact, I am not sure if I will ever go back to the house. Too painful."

"I don't blame you," Brynne said. "Screw him and the house. You'll have money, a lot of money. Buy a place out here by me." She looked at me. "For now though, this being followed business is crazy and needs to stop. Restraining order is the first thing you need, if you ask me."

"We can ask for a restraining order, but the police have stacks of domestic cases all because a spouse violated a restraining order."

"Johnny, I can't live like this. We can't go out. We're trapped here. Get me to a safe place, Brynne too, and we'll figure the rest. Can you do that?"

"Sure. I can. What about other family, though? Out of town or something?"

"No, out of the question. This is my business."

"Fair enough. I'll find a place for you while we get the proof you need."

I finished off my drink and stood. The scenery was always pleasant with these two, and I was craving a second G&T, but there was work. "You have food here?"

"We're stocked. The pantry and the bar." She waved a hand at the TV. "This gets three hundred channels so we have plenty to keep us entertained."

"Anything weird or out of the ordinary, call me. Don't answer the door for anyone."

Brynne let me out the front. I stopped and gazed around at the picturesque setting. *The rich have the same problems as everyone else.* Except theirs looks better, smells better, and tastes better.

My cheating spouse case had a whole new depth of flavor. Someone tailed Ainsley; that I confirmed. Mary Ann was run off the road, the police confirmed. Now, if she was correct, someone followed her in broad daylight. I pulled down the driveway and turned for the city. Too many unknowns on this job to ignore simple safety precautions.

I made a phone call.

17

A mini command center was now set up in my condo, at least for the immediate future. The future being the life expectancy of this case. Katie and I arranged a portable table in my living room and ran a couple of extension cords for our computers.

Eric was on time at eight and George followed in right behind. When I met with Mary Ann and Brynne earlier in the day, I had missed George's call during the lunch hour. He left a message saying he was out of the BST building—said he could not use the phone inside—and sounded scared and nervous. He was upset I did not answer, called back at five o'clock on his drive home, and eagerly agreed to meet at my condo that evening.

"The universe might explode when Eric and George Ainsley are together in this room. Talk about a clash of personalities and cultures," Katie said.

"The entertainment value will be worth the price of admission. I'm also keeping a bottle of bourbon close by."

"I second that."

George's apprehension and skepticism fueled the initial meeting between the two, until George witnessed Eric's fingers flying over the keyboard, pulling up sites that I did not know existed. George was enthralled and they were instant colleagues. The odd pairing of the old school scientist and the genius neo-punk cyber geek.

"Can't find anything on this chick," Eric said.

Eric's failure to find anything on Keira gave George a sense of validation. "Told you. See, I told you. Nothing exists on her, especially before her college years." He got up from the table and paced around the room with his hands clasped behind his back.

"Georgie boy here is correct, boss." Eric moved from dude to boss. "Now what do we do?"

George sat back down. "We hack into the company and her files."

"Whoa, daddy. No can do on the hack."

"What? Why? That's why you're here."

Eric turned to me and I jumped in. "George, he is one of the smartest hackers in the world. We know it, and so does the government. If the feds catch him, then—"

"One way ticket to Janesville for me."

George pushed his chair back from the table, putting space between him and Eric as if he was contagious. "You did time in prison?"

"Afraid so."

"Delarosa, you brought in a criminal?" George was on his feet again. "This was a terrible idea. Goddam terrible idea. I'm leaving. I'll handle all this myself."

"Hold on, George. Let's talk this through," I said, but it was Katie to the rescue.

"Drink, anyone?" She held up the bottle of bourbon like a spokesmodel on a game show.

"Hell, yeah. I thought you were never going to open that." Eric jumped up.

"Perfect idea. Let's have a drink and regroup. George?"

Ainsley hesitated, took a handkerchief from his pants pocket, dabbed his brow. He took a deep breath. "Double, one ice cube."

"Georgie boy, my man. I knew I liked you." Eric served.

We sat around the kitchen table, no computers, and talked. George added details about the space-based solar program and Eric's eyes lit up.

"This is James Bond shit. Ultra-cool, but it will be layered with firewall after firewall."

"I'll do it," George said. "Teach me. That way you are out of it."

"Too dangerous. They catch you, you're in my old bunk at Janesville." Eric poured a round of refills.

My curiosity could not wait any longer. "Eric, how did you survive prison? Your type doesn't last too long in a place like that."

"Easy. My second day there, I asked the guard who was the baddest dude in the joint. He told me, Oscar Ruiz. So, I requested a meeting with Ruiz and everyone thought I was crazy and it was suicide. Ruiz agrees to meet, and I told him I wanted protection in exchange for a favor. He thought I was crazy, too, but said I had balls for trying. That night they snuck me into the computer lab and I changed his mother's credit score to 720 so she could qualify for a mortgage, and also moved some cash into his girlfriend's bank account."

"Damn, dude." Katie gave him a fist bump. "Where did you move the cash from?"

He wagged a finger at her and smiled. "From that day forward, nobody in the place even dared look at me. I was untouchable. If it wasn't for that idea, though, they would have passed me from cell to cell. I'm a genius. The only card-carrying member of Mensa to do time in a federal pen and play punk grunge."

I raised my glass. "Genius is right. So what do we do about this situation?"

"Review. G-dude, what do you want and what do you need?"

It took George a moment to recover from being called G-dude. "I want her out of the company, out of Tom's life, and out of my life. I wish it was back to the way it was before she came along. What I need is her top-secret clearance revoked before we lose the contract."

"From the DOD's perspective, is anything wrong or illegal?" I asked.

"Attempted murder on my niece."

Eric tuned in to my line of thought, paranoia aside. "G-dude, this Keira wants the company, which means she wants the money and the glory. She wants Mrs. Bellamy to disappear so she has Tommy boy to herself, and you are getting in the way."

"Yes."

"And PI Dude here confirmed someone is following you..." He poured himself another drink. "Don't worry; I think better when I'm juiced."

"Me too." Katie splashed more in her glass.

"G-dude, the company will be protected. Cyber security safeguards, all that. I'm not sure what to tell you at this point. I told super PI here that I'm all in, but I don't know how to help. I dig you're upset she sexed up Tommy to score the company loot, but other than that..."

George sank back in his chair, defeated. "They follow me."

"No doubt you have her worried. You're in her way. I say you stay above-board and go legal. Hire a lawyer, go to the DOD. Get out in front of this," I added. "Forget the clandestine route."

"Something to think about. Either way, they'll cut me out."

"Not necessarily. PI is right. Tell them you hired a lawyer and the next step is to bring in government auditors."

I nodded to Eric. *Impressive.* "George, he's right. Other ways to go here."

George thought for a second, and then threw back the remainder of his bourbon. "At least the bourbon was decent."

I handed him the bottle. "Go home, get some sleep. This is not over. I'm here to help. We'll talk in a day or two."

Ainsley left, dejected, and we all felt helpless and sorry for him. He had genuine concerns, but Eric was right—not in my scope of work.

"G-dude has a legit beef, but it's all sort of a bad TV movie, right, dude?"

"Right, dude."

I opened another bottle of bourbon and poured. Eric and I sat on the sofa and I allowed him to quiz me nonstop about PI work. Despite the outward appearance, he could talk with extreme intelligence on many topics, and I think we covered them all. He could also drink. We were doing a pro job on the bourbon when Katie had opened her laptop for one more GPS check.

"They moved. Both cars are parked at an address right off the interstate. I'm checking the maps."

"This the woman and Bellamy?" Eric asked. "Damn."

"Let's hope," I said.

"A motel off Exit 29. Are we going?" Katie jumped up.

"Yep."

"Wait for me. Bathroom first," she said.

Eric threw on his jacket. "This is rockin'. PIs in action."

I grabbed my camera bag from the closet. "You're not going."

"What? I'm part of the team."

"Where is your car?"

"In the alley."

"You can go with us to your car. Thanks for coming tonight. I appreciate it. We'll send you a check. Katie?"

"I'm here." She grabbed the laptop and we hustled down the stairs, ran through McNally's drawing stares and turning heads, including Mike's.

"Hey."

We went through the kitchen door into the alley.

"Boss, dude, please. This is cool time."

"Not tonight. You're a smart guy, would like to have you around. We'll talk."

"All right. Later, dude." He walked to his car and yelled over his shoulder. "I'm disappointed."

"What did you just say to him?" Katie asked.

"Can we go?" I opened the garage door. A flash at the end of the alley caught my eye. *Headlights*. A car barreled toward us.

A second car turned in from the opposite end of the alley. The headlights were blinding.

Eric ran over to us. "Dude, this better not be for me."

The first car pulled to us and stopped. The door flung open and a granite block of a man got out with a gun drawn. The second car angled in and a woman hopped out with her gun on us.

"Johnny?" Katie said.

The man came around his car. "FBI. Don't move."

18

The man came forward. "Delarosa?"

"Who's asking?"

"Don't be cute. Turn around, hands against the building."

We complied and the male agent made quick work of relieving me of my Beretta, then he frisked Katie while the female agent gave Eric a pat-down.

"My name is Special Agent Quade and this is Special Agent Ortiz," he said. "Is there a place we can talk? Inside?"

"My place, upstairs. Need to go around the building or through the bar," I said.

"Through the bar. Let's go."

We paraded through McNally's again. Mike could smell a federal agent from a hundred yards away. He mouthed to me, "You okay?"

I nodded. I feared Eichenberg would start a protest, but the first lesson you learned in the joint: keep your mouth shut. He did.

We went into my condo and Quade put Katie and Eric on the sofa with Ortiz standing guard, and took me out to the hall. Smart to divide us.

"George Ainsley your client?"

"No."

"Try again?"

"He did not hire me."

"Why is he here?"

"Mind telling me what this is about?"

He leveled his eyes and sized me up. I faced off with federal agents many times in my career, but never against one like this. I'm six one; he had two inches on me and had to be a rock-solid two-twenty, with a V-shaped back, not an ounce of fat on his body, and arms the size of my thighs. If that was not enough, he had steel-blue eyes, close-cropped black hair, and a square leading-man jaw, as if he walked off the pages of a men's fitness magazine.

"I'll tell you, Delarosa, but I need you to be on the right side of this."

"I'll try, but I'm in the dark."

"Tell me about Ainsley."

"Contacted me, but what he wants can't happen. You've been following him. You got him scared and paranoid."

"He's in way over his head. We're keeping an eye so he doesn't bury himself."

"How so?"

"He's raised red flags all over Washington. Pings at NSA, CIA, DOD, and Justice. Drew attention to himself. Got us curious, especially from a guy at this point in his career—stellar reputation, close to retirement. His actions don't add up. Then he hires you. What did he want?"

"Why do I get the sense you already know what he wanted?"

"You had direct contact, gives us third-party confirmation. We're aware of the concerns he has with Bellamy Space, and we also know Mary Ann Bellamy is your client."

"Well, well. Big brother is watching."

He shrugged. "Blame Ainsley."

"He was jacked about the affair between Bellamy and the woman. I'm sure you are aware." He nodded. "Said it was going to ruin everything. Wanted me to hack into the company, dig into her, and discredit her. Bordered on conspiracy theory a bit, but with a payday on the horizon, I figured he's smoked about getting cut out."

He made a note on a pad he pulled from his pocket. "Eichenberg?"

"Eyes on him, too?"

"We all do. He breathes next to computer and we get a hit."

"Friend of my assistant. We brought him in to convince Ainsley that what he wanted to do was impossible. Ainsley left here tonight dejected, but he understood."

"Yeah, Eichenberg showing up here definitely got our attention. Smart. Let's hope it worked."

"Why the dramatic stop and frisk? Could have just knocked."

"C'mon, Delarosa. Keep the subject off-balance. Interviewing skills 101."

So far, Agent Quade had yet to irritate me. "Fair enough. Now what?"

"Back inside."

Katie and Eric both stood and Ortiz took a step toward us when Quade and I walked back into the condo. Katie's eyes were huge with questions.

"Relax," Quade said. "You two, sit back down." Katie and Eric looked to me, and I nodded. "We apologize for the delay. Mr. Delarosa and I here had a productive conversation." We pulled chairs in from the kitchen and we all sat around and listened as Quade gave a brief recap of how and why Ainsley popped on their radar. Katie did not blink once as he talked. Her eyes were fixated on the All-American boy. I could tell she was calculating how many children they were going to have and when. "The reason we are here tonight is to ask you, the three of you, to work for us."

"To do what?" Eric asked.

"What you do best."

Eric stood. "No way, dude."

Quade held up his hand. "I need to get approval from my superiors, but if this goes as I want, you'll have full immunity for the scope of this job. In writing."

"I'm not crazy, dude. No thank you. Am I free to leave?"

"Of course."

He stopped at me. "PI Dude—good luck." Exit Eric.

"Plus Katie is leaving on vacation tomorrow, so I'm afraid my ranks are dwindling."

"It was canceled." Katie's face blushed. "I forgot to tell you. Mandy got sick. So I'm available to work whenever you want, Agent...what is it again?"

"Quade."

"Yes, Agent Quade. Delarosa Investigations is here for whatever you need. Always happy to help out fellow law enforcement."

Ortiz rolled her eyes. "Quade, we done?" She was Hispanic, mid-thirties, medium height, more muscles than curves, had a cute, round face, light-brown eyes, and short brown hair.

He turned to me. "Can we stop by in the morning? Ten?"

"Sure, we'll talk. Always willing to help out fellow law enforcement," I said.

Katie's face turned a shade of red I had not seen before.

They left and she threw herself on the sofa and buried her head in a cushion and screamed. "I am such a dork."

"Trip is canceled, huh?"

She popped up. "No wedding ring either."

"Smitten, are we?"

"My panties melted when he frisked me...electricity shot through my body." She paced around the condo like a madwoman. "Johnny, I think it's love at first sight."

"How about you come back to reality and we go to work."

"What?"

"Bellamy and the blonde at the motel. Remember? Or did your mind melt, too?"

She grabbed her jacket and the computer.

"Mandy will kill me."

19

The Starry Night Motel was a roadside roach trap connected to the truck stop fifteen miles north of Port City on I-64. The portable GPS trackers we had on both Bellamy's and the blonde's cars, still showed them at the motel. I hoped to grab some shots of them coming out of their love nest to give Mary Ann the proof she needed, which was the reason she hired me. The George Ainsley business with the FBI was intriguing, and Quade and Ortiz must have something substantial or they would not be following around a paranoid old-timer, but I preferred they come back tomorrow with a check in hand. No pro-bono here.

"The indicators are moving." Katie focused on the computer while I drove. "Their date must be over."

"Damn. I wanted to take their picture."

"Bellamy is heading toward the interstate...Keira's car stopped. She is still at the Starry Night."

I made the last ten miles in eight minutes. The motel connected to the truck stop by an access road where eighteen-wheelers lined up end-to-end for the night.

"Duck down a bit. Your hair is a giveaway. We need to hide it," I said.

She slid down in the seat as I made a slow recon pass of the place. "I see it. The Mercedes," Katie said.

Keira's car was not close to the motel, but out in the lot by itself; as if she was leaving then changed her mind and backed up. "Anyone in the car with her?"

"No. She's alone."

To make a U-turn at this spot in the road could draw attention, so I had no choice but to continue to the truck stop to turn around. It was the usual several acre mash of diesel pumps, a restaurant, convenience store, and shower facilities for the truckers. I pulled to the far end of the lot, away from the traffic. I hopped out and got a black ski cap from the trunk for Katie. Somehow, she hid her massive blonde mane under the cap.

"Perfect. Let's find a spot to keep an eye on our girl."

"Don't bother. She's headed this way." We watched the screen as the blinking cursor moved in our direction. "You think she saw us?"

"No. I doubt it."

"She could have seen us the other night, after the restaurant."

"Unlikely. There she is." Keira's Mercedes drove on the lot and by the grace of some private eye god, went to the opposite end. We were a hundred yards away from her with a decent line of sight, except for being interrupted every time a truck pulled in or out.

Katie grabbed the binoculars from the back. "She stopped. Might be texting."

I snapped a telephoto lens on my Nikon for my own glimpse. "What's she up to? Not exactly the kind of place I would expect to find her. You keep on her." I set the camera down, picked up the laptop, and switched screens to Bellamy's tracker. The cursor pinged a few miles from North Shore and his cozy bed.

"Some girl is going to the car."

I put the camera to my eye. A skinny girl in tiny jeans shorts, black hair, and a tube top walked up to Keira's car.

"Johnny, a drug deal. You think Keira is buying drugs?"

"No. A lizard."

"What?"

"The girl is a lot lizard. Truck stop hooker."

"No way. That is gross."

A semi pulled from the pumps and blocked our view for a few seconds. When the truck passed, the girl was in a dead run from the car and disappeared between two rigs.

"Whatever she said, the girl looked scared to death." Keira sat and we sat. We took turns on watch, switching every five minutes. "I can't believe you are not going on your vacation."

"Not now. We have a chance to work with the FBI. I can't leave."

"You got Agent Quade on the brain."

"Shut up."

Fifteen minutes later, a small white sedan with two yellow lights mounted on top appeared and turned in our direction. "Please no."

"Is it security?"

"Hide the camera and binoculars. We're suspicious over here by ourselves. He'll think I got myself a lot lizard." The car pulled up and the driver shined a flashlight at us. "Don't say a word." I lowered my window.

He peered at us from under his cap. "You two okay?"

"We are. Needed a driving break." He held the light on Katie, to determine whether he recognized her or whether she was under duress.

"Might want to move up closer to the building. Bunch of crazies around here at night."

"Right. Will do. Thanks."

He moved on.

"What was that about?" Katie asked.

"Trafficking or prostitution. Places like this are rampant. Doing his job."

She put the binoculars back on Keira. "Johnny."

I used the camera. A white paneled van had pulled in and parked behind Keira's car. She and two men were standing, huddled together. One man was tall and skinny, the other short with a moustache. Both with black hair. "We need sound from now on." I snapped a few pictures of the group and zoomed in on the license plate.

"We can do that?"

The huddle broke and both men stepped away and stood with their backs against the van. Keira appeared to be berating them. The skinny guy took a step forward, animated, his arms flailing. With one swift motion, Keira flicked open an asp baton and struck him on his knee. He let go of a yelp that we heard, and crumbled to the ground.

"Did you see that?"

"Asp baton. Police carry them. Quite effective, I would say." The moustache man knelt to tend to his partner while Keira opened the trunk of the Mercedes and came back with a black object in her hand. Moustache stood to face her just as she thrust the object into his gut. His body doubled over and he fell limp to the pavement.

"She shot him, Johnny. Oh my God, she shot him."

"Stun gun. She hit him with a stunner."

She stood over both men like a conquering hero, and then kicked the skinny guy twice in his ribs. He writhed on the ground while she waved the stun gun in his face, emphasizing her point, and then got back in her car and peeled off. She flew out so fast it took the GPS almost a minute to catch up. She was on the interstate headed toward the city.

Tall, blonde, and brutal. If she could stick a stun gun in a man's gut, she would have no problem sending goons to run a woman off the road. *Did she just punish them for a botched job on Mary Ann?*

***

The events of the evening had me too keyed up to go to bed. I poured a slug of bourbon in a glass and took it to the balcony of my condo. The twinkling lights of Port City blanketed out before me and I wondered how many other brutal, violent acts were taking place at the truck stops, in the gritty back alleys, the filthy crack houses, or in the posh mini-mansions of North Shore. I wondered whether there was enough love in the city to offset the inhumane ways humans treat one another.

The safe house was now a priority. I sent a text message and received a response in thirty seconds: the house was ready.

The threat level on this case was now raised to vicious.

20

She did not want to go to the safe house without Brynne and stood firm in her protest. I did not think it necessary to subject Brynne to a potentially dangerous situation, but neither woman would take no for an answer.

"She's my only support. Besides, I am not staying in some house by myself," Mary Ann said.

"You will not be by yourself. Security will be there with you."

"No thanks."

Brynne came into the kitchen of her home with two overnight bags. "Let's go."

"Johnny doesn't want you to go."

"Why? I'm going."

"Brynne, I cannot put you in any type of potential harm, especially when it has nothing to do with you."

"Mary Ann is my best friend. If you are moving her, then I'm going."

"I don't know how long this will take. A day or two, maybe a week."

"Nothing for me to do here but play tennis and drink wine. Will there be wine wherever you are taking us?"

"Yes, whatever you want."

"I fail to see a problem."

The women stood in defiance, with their arms folded across their chest. I knew better, but I would not win the argument and I wanted both out of Brynne's house.

***

We drove twenty miles south of Crescent Beach to the northern edge of the beachfront state park, to a massive, modern oceanfront house. The proximity to the state park prohibited any new development in the area, setting the house in quiet isolation. The nearest neighbor was a quarter mile north, the beach was to the east, and to the west was the old coastal highway. A search of property records showed the owners of the house as Enterprise Holdings, LLC, as ambiguous as a name could be.

The house had private beach access, three sun decks, one covered deck, four levels, five bedrooms, two outdoor showers, a fully stocked modern kitchen, three wet bars, a family room with a sixty-five-inch television, parking for three cars, high-speed wireless, and—most important—two security guards.

Emmanuel Blackmon met us in the driveway. "Johnny. Been a while." He was one of the "strong arms," as she called them. He was just under six feet tall, and a solid block of muscle. A former Army Ranger, spent time as a private mercenary, he now worked exclusively for my contact. His father was African American, his mother Israeli, giving him light-brown skin and hazel eyes. Receiving attention from the ladies was never a problem for him, but he only dealt with women on his terms. A man's man, he was not one of those insecure wimps who always needed a woman around.

"Emmanuel. Looking good, as usual."

"I try."

I introduced them as Mrs. Bellamy and Mrs. Middleton but they quickly corrected me and told Emmanuel to call them by their first names. I took it as an attempt to ditch any attachment to husbands present and former, especially in front of Emmanuel.

He led us into the house and they marveled at the modern, beach décor. Mary Ann and Brynne, even with their affluence, were in awe. I was too. It went through some upgrades since my last visit.

I took over a cottage on Crescent Beach in a leftover divorce deal with my ex-wife, but my place looked like a single-wide on concrete blocks compared to this showstopper. The girls wandered out to the deck.

"A safe house is supposed to be functional, Emmanuel. Not opulent."

"You know how she is."

"Yes, I do." Mary Ann and Brynne were snapping pictures with their cell phones. I brought them back inside. "Give me your phones." They did and I removed the batteries while they protested. "For your safety."

"I can't be without my phone," Brynne said.

"I can take you back to your house. The decision is yours. If you want to stay, fine, but there are rules."

We all sat around on sofas in the great room. "You'll be safe in the house." I checked to Emmanuel. "How many other guys?"

"Two of us at all times unless you tell me different."

"The batteries are out of your phones because they can be tracked. I don't mean to scare you, but, Mary Ann, I believe the attempt on you was real. I want to keep you safe and this is how we do it. Emmanuel will supply a phone if you need, but keep that to a minimum. The house is stocked with anything you need. Think of it this way: a few days of luxury, hidden away from the world. Who wouldn't want this, right?"

"The hell with my phone. I don't want to talk to anyone anyway." Brynne put her feet up on the coffee table.

Mary Ann did not look as convinced. "All this trouble because of my husband's nonsense. I'm so embarrassed. Who pays for all this?"

"Your husband, of course." That brought a smile. "A few more things. You do whatever Emmanuel or the other men tell you. You will not be able to leave the house. Mary Ann, your husband already thinks you are at Brynne's. You each will use Emmanuel's phone and call your kids and tell them you had an opportunity to get away for a week, and you're in a house in the mountains without any cell service."

"What about my Uncle George?"

"Taken care of. I'll keep him close." My lips stay sealed about Ainsley until my meeting with Quade.

"Please do. I am so worried about him."

"Don't worry, sit back, and relax. Take a deep breath. I will check in on a regular basis."

"I'm so nervous about all this."

Brynne jumped up. "To the bar."

"Whatever you are making, make Mary Ann one too," I said.

Emmanuel followed me outside and introduced me to his partner on the job, Jamal Collingsworth, a broad-shouldered African American, about six two, without an ounce of fat on his body.

I shook his hand. "Former Ranger?"

"Yes sir."

"You guys work out all the time?"

"Only seven days a week, sir," Jamal said.

"Best I can do is bend my elbow."

They laughed.

"We do pretty good with that, too, sir."

"What's the deal?" Emmanuel asked.

"Somebody ran Mary Ann off the road the other night. Bad divorce going down. She claims it was a white van, but no other leads. Then, last night, I think I saw the same cats. White cargo van, two Caucasians, one with a moustache. Keep an eye out. They work for a tall blonde, drives a black Mercedes, mean as hell. I watched her stick a stun gun in the gut of one of her flunkies."

"Amateurs. Easy money."

"We're playing it safe. I don't like the vibe on this one. Check in every four hours?"

"Standard protocol." He walked me to my car. "She wants you to stop by tonight."

"Oh yeah?" I got in the car. "Keep an eye on the tall one. She could get playful on you."

"I keep it all business."

"Smart man."

21

Y ou want what?" asked George Ainsley.

"Information," Quade said.

Ainsley got up from his seat and walked over to the window of the fifth-story hotel room of the downtown Port City Hilton. He stared at the cityscape for a minute while Quade and I sat, not saying a word.

After witnessing Keira Kaine's brutality the night before, I called Quade and requested we move the meeting to a safer location later in the day. I sent Ainsley a message on the burner phone and he replied he could meet us at noon. Quade agreed, and as a precaution, even did a bug sweep of the hotel room. I thought that was overkill, but better to be safe. It also gave me time to situate Mary Ann in the safe house.

Quade and I met thirty minutes before Ainsley arrived and he briefed me on the plan he cooked up. Plus, he provided more background on Keira Kaine, and why she got the attention of the FBI.

Ainsley came back to the small table and sat down. "Why, again?"

"Your suspicions about Keira might be correct, but when you started digging into her background, alarm bells rang all over Washington. You were investigating a senior executive at a defense contractor on a top-secret clearance. You got our attention," said Quade. "That's why we followed you. Then we heard about Bellamy's wife, your niece, understood your motivation, and we came forward. Now you can help us and maybe get the satisfaction you want."

"I had to do something. She is destroying our company."

"Your instincts were not unfounded; I only wish you contacted us first. Her name has come up before."

"How so?"

"I can't say. Classified, but Mr. Ainsley, trust me, it is important or we would not ask this of you." Ainsley nodded. "If you agree to help us, you acknowledge you could be putting yourself in danger."

"Of course. I cannot allow her to steal everything that I, that Tom and I, built. These are lifetime accomplishments...a life's passion, to be...to be thrown away because of a sick, tawdry love affair. I can't sit back and do nothing."

Quade stood, paced around for a second, then put both hands on the table and leaned close to Ainsley. A common technique that put the interviewer in a power position.

"Mr. Ainsley, it's extremely important that you answer this next question honestly, or the entire plan does not work. Did you tell anyone, anyone at all, that you went to see Johnny, or that Mary Ann hired him?"

"No, no one."

"You didn't tell Bellamy?"

"No, I swear. There is nobody else I can even talk to. No other family and I don't trust anyone at the company."

"No company gossip? Water cooler chatter?"

"I overhear company gossip. Everyone loves a sex scandal, but nobody includes me."

I got up and refilled our coffee cups. I did not make habit of cooperating with the feds, but I liked Quade's plan, and I had to admit, it provided some work with a much-needed edge.

Quade continued. "All we need is for you to be the eyes and ears inside the building."

"I can do that."

"Do Keira and Bellamy ever go out to lunch together?"

"Every day. They go to a place called Lulu's Café. Not too far from our building."

"How do you know?"

"Everyone knows. Some of the women in the office will go there so they can spot Tom and Keira then gossip about it later."

We talked through what we wanted from him. Information on their routines and what he could expect from us.

"Meanwhile, keep to your normal, daily routine. We will contact you on the phone Johnny gave you. Keep the phone in your car; check it at lunch time and in the evening."

Ainsley stood and shook our hands. "It is the right thing to do, isn't it?"

"Yes, George, it is. One day soon, I'll explain," Quade said.

***

Ainsley left and Quade made a call. Five minutes later, Agent Ortiz came into the hotel room with Eric Eichenberg.

"The boy wonder. We meet again," I said.

"Dude, what are you doing here? They came and got me at my job. I freaked."

"Sit down."

We sat around the table again and Quade put a sheet of paper in front of Eric. "This is a document giving you full immunity for any work you do for us on the case. You will also receive compensation of twenty-five hundred dollars. One-time payment, in cash, untaxable, untraceable."

Eichenberg's eyes went from Quade to me. "For what?"

"Need you to create a legend for Johnny, then do deep web research on a person we have under surveillance."

"Don't you guys have an entire FBI to do this stuff?"

"We do, but it would take me weeks to get done what you can do in a day. How about we sign the paper?"

He turned to me. "Am I helping you on this? 'Cause I'll only do this for you."

"You are."

"A legend, a complete background?"

"Yes. Work history, credit report, addresses, schools, the works. I will give you details, plus a Social Security number for him," Quade said.

"What's the catch, fed dude?"

"The catch is we have national security interests to protect and you are the best person for this job."

"PI Dude?"

"You'll be fine. Do what you do, computer dude."

"Where will I work?"

"Right here. We'll supply everything. Plus, unlimited room service. Agent Ortiz will stay with you."

He glanced around the room, took it all in, gave Agent Ortiz a quick once-over. "Quade, as long as it's your ass that goes down and not mine."

22

Two clients on one case is one client too many, and I never expected the FBI to be a client. I dealt with many federal agents over my career and navigating the egos and arrogance was the constant frustration. They never wanted input from the city cops walking the beat, but Quade seemed to put his ego aside and realized the benefit in my involvement. I gave him credit for that because Keira Kaine would smell a fed from miles away. Still, my sixth sense was my most loyal ally and it reminded me to only trust myself. Quade had a plan, but I damn sure needed one, too.

Only a few days ago, I complained to Jim Rosswell about taking on another routine cheating spouse case. Now, the opposite was on my plate. The brutality I witnessed, as delivered by Keira Kaine, and Ainsley's contention that she had nefarious ambitions, were not lost on me. The furtive aspect with Quade was an adrenaline spike, but my first loyalty was to client number one, Mary Ann Bellamy, and securing proof of the affair.

McNally's was between lunch and happy hour, which gave me a chance to gather my troop—Mike. We sat in my back booth and I filled him in on Ainsley, the

FBI, at which he cringed—no love lost there—and Eric Eichenberg creating a legend for me.

"You are going undercover for them? Why?"

"Curiosity."

"Suddenly you're an adventure seeker? No way. I need a drink to listen to this." He got up, grabbed a bottle from the bar, and came back and poured two drinks. "Brunette or blonde?"

"Why do you always go there?"

"Well?"

I threw back my bourbon and poured another. "Blonde. I watched her put a hurt on two guys and it got me curious."

"Now you have a pain fetish?"

"No, but I feel for the wife and the old man."

"Feelings? I'm worried about you."

"Something with the blonde, though. Why would an executive with an aerospace firm, government contractor with a top-secret clearance, be meeting with two low lifes at a truck stop motel? The feds are on to something with her and I think they are right. She's bad. I'm not sure how, but my curiosity is piqued." I lifted my glass to my summary.

"You got a point. Feds give you details?"

"A few. Another meeting this afternoon."

"Let's see. Top-secret clearance, government contractor. She's compromised." He raised his glass and toasted his expert deduction.

"We're going to find out."

"Please don't get yourself killed and leave me to run this joint by myself. Next thing you know, we'll be holding a memorial golf tournament in your honor to raise money for some charity and I'm not into that." He finished his drink and got up from the booth. "Let me know how I can help."

Katie came in and Mike stopped dead in his tracks. "Damn, where are you going?"

She wore navy-blue dress slacks, heels, a cream-colored blouse, dangling gold earrings, a necklace to match, full make up, and her hair was down and flowing in head-turning, show-stopping curls.

"I'm coming here, to work."

"Did you forget this is a bar? Not some upscale, five-star restaurant. You look fantastic, but a bit over-dressed, wouldn't you say?" Mike said.

"No, just tired of jeans and T-shirts every day."

"In that case, the grease traps need cleaned out."

They stared at each other for a moment, and then Mike pointed at me. "She's your employee today."

"Smart man, Mr. McNally," Katie said. He walked away shaking his head as she sat in the booth. "What's on the schedule?"

"What if the grease traps do need to be cleaned?"

"Change of clothes in my car."

"Uh, huh." I cocked an eyebrow.

"C'mon. What are we doing?"

"You'll find out." I got up. "You coming?"

"Yes. Will Scott be there?"

"Scott? Who is Scott?"

"Don't be a jerk."

***

Agent Quade hit the Hilton lobby the same time we did and we all rode the elevator to the fifth floor without anyone saying a word. I did catch him taking a second glance at Katie.

He tapped twice on the room door. Agent Ortiz opened it and we went in. Eric was at the table and jumped to his feet when he saw Katie. "Damn, girl. You are smokin'."

She blushed. "Thanks."

"What are you doing here?"

Quade said, "Yes, what is she doing here?"

"I want her up to speed on this. She's part of the deal."

Quade assessed for a second, used the opportunity to look her over. "Fine. I prefer she stay here, not in the field."

Quade, Eric, and I sat around the table and Katie and Ortiz sat on the sofa. Eric gave me the details on my new persona. "You are now Arthur Rhodes from California." He handed me a sheet that listed my Social Security number, an address in San Jose, details of my education, name of a former wife, and two previous addresses. He also gave me a California driver's license, complete with my picture.

"This is impressive. All in one day," I said.

"Dude, Mamacita Maria here is off the chain amazing." We all turned toward Ortiz and it was now her turn to blush. "Right, Mama?"

"Umm..." She cleared her throat. "Yes, we were able to pull this together in record time. You also have a credit history if they check, and I'm sure they will."

Quade tapped the paper. "Learn this overnight and I say we make an attempt tomorrow at lunch at the café Ainsley mentioned. You sure you're comfortable doing this?"

"Been many years since an undercover assignment. I'm up for it."

He reached a hand to Ortiz. "The phone?"

She handed me a burner phone. "Use only this to communicate with us. It also has a separate GPS so we can track you." She opened an envelope and gave me a small, white disk, the size of a button on a man's dress shirt. "Hide this in your clothes. A second tracker, in case it all blows up."

"So you can find my body?"

Neither agent reacted. They had traded their sense of humor for a badge.

For once, I hoped Eric would talk, but Katie broke the awkward silence with an equally awkward comment. "So, Scott, will I be here with you, or in the field with Johnny? Either way is fine. I'm working on my PI license, so any experience is great for me."

Ortiz turned away, suppressing a smile. Quade, to his credit, did not embarrass her. "We'll figure out your role in the operation."

"How long does it take to get a PI license?" Eric asked.

"Eric, how about we stay focused?"

"Right, PI boss. I got it."

We went through the approach for tomorrow. I explained how I wanted to play it and Quade agreed. If Keira and Bellamy did not keep their lunch date, we wait another day. Quade made clear his goal in contacting her. "Let's hope she reacts. Do not engage in any other conversation."

"Understood."

"We meet back here after."

Eric stretched out on the bed, Quade was first out of the room, and Ortiz stepped in front of Katie. "Sweetie, many women have tried and all have failed. He is all business. Trust me."

Eric called after Ortiz. "Mamacita Maria, remember my gig next Saturday."

Ortiz's eyes went to the floor and she wasted no time on her exit.

Katie flopped her head back on the sofa. "Was I obvious?"

"Katie, babe, you took a shot and missed," Eric said. "It's cool. C'mon, I have room service." He patted the bed. "Anything we want. We can party all night."

"Oh my God." She got up, grabbed her purse, and scrammed.

I said to Eric, "Hey, you took a shot and missed."

He shrugged and picked up the remote.

23

The McNally's-sponsored police league softball team kept the bar busy all night. They won the championship and Mike had the beer taps wide open in celebration. Katie and I both pitched in, me behind the bar and she in the kitchen, and we took turns checking the GPS on the laptop for any movement of Bellamy's Range Rover or Keira's Mercedes. Nothing tawdry so far, each parked at their respective houses all evening.

A nervous tic about George Ainsley crept into my gut. I worried about him as our eyes and ears in the company, and whether he could handle the task without Keira growing wise to his efforts to wedge between her and Bellamy. I needed him to play it cool and not be overzealous.

I sent a text message asking him to meet me at Nancy's at 7:00 a.m. for breakfast the next morning. I received back a quick, "*Yes.*"

Around 9:30, the softball team and their wives and girlfriends dwindled out and I began to wipe down the bar when Katie yelled from the back.

"It moved." Her frantic hand motioned for me.

I hurried to the booth and the GPS cursor for Keira's car was now on the interstate headed toward the same truck stop from the other night. "Only her car. Bellamy's is still at his house."

"Do you want to follow?"

"Of course." She threw off her apron.

I sent another quick text. She grabbed the laptop, and ten minutes later, we pulled under the portico of the downtown Hilton. "What are we doing?" Katie asked. "She's on the highway."

"You'll see."

Two minutes later, Scott Quade hustled out of the hotel lobby, still buttoning his shirt. "Why didn't you tell me?" She flipped down the visor and checked her face. "You owe me. I could have changed."

He squeezed his long body into the backseat of the Buick. "Thanks for including me. Where is she?"

Katie twisted around to Quade and held the laptop for him to see. She pointed at the GPS cursor, which was on the interstate.

"She's headed toward the motel and the truck stop where we observed her before."

Quade asked a few questions about us being here the other night but we did not have much to add. Katie watched the cursor on the screen and we figured she stopped at the Starry Night. We took the exit off the interstate and slowed as we approached the motel. Eighteen-wheelers lined the access road again and we used them for cover, sliding into a spot between two trucks. We had a clear view of the motel parking lot.

"There's her car," Katie said. "And the van. Scott, we suspect it's the same van that ran Mary Ann Bellamy off the road."

He nodded. "Good to know. Do you have binoculars?"

"Of course." She handed them back to him.

"Katie, your hair. Do you have the cap?" I said.

She shot me a look that almost took my head off, but relented when Quade agreed it was a smart idea to hide her hair.

"Don't want to give them anything they can recognized." I watched Quade in the rearview mirror as he watched her tuck her hair inside the ski cap. *Maybe he's not all business after all.*

We waited forty-five minutes in almost complete silence except for Katie asking Scott questions about his personal life. She could not help herself. *Where he went to school, where he was from, did he like sports.* He was polite and answered all she asked, but never asked her anything. I sensed her discomfort and embarrassment.

Quade leaned forward. "Can we move closer?"

"You sure we want to?" I said.

"No, but I don't have a clear view of the license tag on the van."

We drove into the lot, Katie with the camera ready, and Quade slouched down in the back seat. We made two passes and she clicked away. I parked as far from her car and the van as possible, but only thirty yards separated us.

A woman—if we could call her that—came out of a motel room and walked across the lot toward the truck stop. She was tall, rail thin, had long, stringy brown hair, wore a blue bikini top and jeans that hung off her skinny hips, and her arms were covered in tattoos.

Katie filled in the rest. "Lot lizard."

"What?" Quade asked.

"Lot lizard. Hookers who work the truck stops. Drugged out, too, I'm sure."

"How do you know that?"

She shrugged. "I'm not as new as I appear."

Another thirty minutes went by and I noticed Katie's eyes going closed. Mine were not far behind. It was after midnight at this point and I was about to call it when a motel room door opened and Keira walked out with her two henchmen behind her.

"Show time, folks."

We came alive. Quade used the binoculars and Katie zoomed in and snapped pictures. We were now close enough to get clear shots of their faces.

"Quade, the box on the floor back there."

He opened it. "Sweet." It contained a small, gun-shaped, battery-powered parabolic microphone. He turned it on, put on the headset and lowered his window, pointing the mic in the direction of the trio. "Does it record?"

"Yes. Squeeze the trigger."

The three stood beside her car and it appeared Keira did most of the talking. Both goons had their hands on their hips, listening and nodding. She jabbed the tall guy in the chest to make a point, and then turned to the short one. He backed up a few steps.

"I'll be damned." Quade took the headset off and picked up the binoculars.

Katie turned to him. "What is it?"

"Interesting. Here, listen."

He handed me the mic. Katie and I shared the headphones and she aimed it toward our target. We heard their voices, but they spoke in another language.

Katie lifted the headphone from her ear. "What is it? Russian or something?"

I turned to Quade. "You know these guys?"

"The tall one might be Maxim Vlasova. Not sure about the other one," he said. "I am assigned to the organized crime unit in New York, but we detected an increase in activity in a cell down here in Port City, so here I am. No doubt they're Bratva."

Katie faced Quade. "Bratva?"

"Russian mob. Quite active in the United States. I'll explain but let's keep our attention on the action."

A beat-down broke out. Keira had her two goons in full retreat. They shuffled backward in a circle while she jockeyed them around like a lioness backing her prey into a snare. Their heads bobbed up and down.

Quade put the headphones on again. "She's laying them out. Something about them not following orders and being where they were supposed to be."

"You speak Russian?" Katie snapped a few more shots.

"No. I understand some basics. Go as close on their faces as you can. I'll run the pictures through facial recognition."

The dress-down stopped and Keira removed two envelopes from her car and handed each man one.

"Payday?"

"Yeah, or instructions, or both."

Keira got into her car and we all ducked down until she was out of the lot. The two men checked the contents of the envelopes as they went back to their motel room.

Quade nodded toward the motel.

"Job for our hacker boy."

"Say no more."

***

We dropped Quade off at the Hilton and Katie and I argued about her involvement in the case. I wanted her out of the field from this point forward. The Russians get one look at her and she was as good as dead—after they used her as a sex toy. Not to mention my demise as well.

She did not speak to me when she got out of the car. I waited until she drove off. She now had standing orders to text me as soon as she was home, and I even cooked up a code name she was to use to make sure she was not texting me out of duress. I would take a quiet and mad Katie over a dead one any day.

A bottle of merlot was already open on the counter in my condo. I poured a glass and gulped it down—not too sophisticated, but it got the alcohol on the fast lane into my system. After a shower, I downloaded eight pictures of the Russians, and one of the license plate of the van, from my camera to my laptop, and emailed them and the sound recording to Quade.

I finished a second and now sipped at a third glass of wine. I put Sinatra on the CD player. I needed Frank to mellow out the evening as I stretched out on the sofa. Photographing cheating husbands was one thing; photographing members of Bratva took the work to a much higher level, a level I did not expect on this case.

The clock clicked to 2:00 a.m. My meeting with Ainsley was at 7:00. He was still an unknown entity and I worried for his safety more than ever. I feared he was in way over his head. The night was now short; my mind was racing, and the wine bottle empty.

"Fly Me to the Moon," took me away for a minute, but sleep would not come that night.

24

Nancy's Diner did a brisk breakfast business but I called ahead and had Nancy reserve me the table in the front window. George Ainsley agreed to meet at 7:00, so I arrived at 6:30 and made a few trips around the block to make sure we did not have any unwanted company. After last night and the revelation of Keira working with the Russian mob, I worried about Ainsley. He had access to everything at BST, and it would take about ten seconds for someone like Vlasova to ply information from him.

It was important for George to stay the course, not react to anything he saw or overheard at the company, and to relay pertinent information back to Quade and me in the manner we dictated. We did not want him to initiate contact, I told him we would contact him and only by the disposable phone. We had to assume Keira had people watching and listening to everything he said and did, and if she was as smart as I thought, it would be business as usual at BST and George would not have any information to report.

She was sharp enough to not give George any reason to challenge her, but the affair with Tom Bellamy was a miscalculation. If she used sex to infiltrate the company, as Ainsley claimed, she made a mistake by allowing him to fall in love and want to divorce his wife. Rule number one in spy tradecraft: do not get emotionally involved with a target. She now had a jilted spouse and an angry co-worker on her plate. If it were not for the late-night meetings with two known members of Bratva, I would leave the whole mess to a love affair gone wrong, take my pictures, and go on to the next job.

Nancy brought me a coffee and I told her I wanted to move to the back table as soon as Ainsley arrived.

"Something has you bothered. I can tell," she said.

I shrugged. "You keep an eye out. For anything."

She patted my shoulder and went to another table. Seven o'clock came and went and my stomach started to crawl. A young man walked into the diner and sat at the end of the counter. He had dark hair, a short scraggly beard, and wore jeans, sandals, and a hooded sweatshirt. He glanced around and then ordered a coffee. I had one eye on the street and one eye on him. Every minute or so, he would turn and scan the restaurant.

My phone beeped. A text from Ainsley. *"Sorry. Traffic."* At the same moment, the door opened and a young woman with green and pink streaks in her blonde hair entered. The man at the counter broke into a smile and stood to greet her, and I was furious I allowed my paranoia to control me.

Five minutes later, a white SUV pulled to the curb and an older man with silver hair got out. I looked at the car and the man again, and it hit me as if I had been shot between the eyes by a solar-powered, space-based microwave beam.

I called Emmanuel.

***

Lulu's Café was one of those fancy, new age vegan places located at the Port City Towne Center, a new retail-dining development a few miles from BST. I took a table in the rear of the restaurant, giving myself a clear view of the door. A menu was on the table and it featured everything tofu. Tofu burgers, grilled tofu, salad with tofu, and a tofu dessert. I was tempted to crack a joke and ask for a cheeseburger and a beer.

A rather large girl—with a round, pimply face, "Brenda" on her nametag, and the personality of a chunk of tofu—came to take my order. She did not greet me, smile, or look me in the eye, and by her appearance, I do not think she ate what she served. I ordered a salad with Italian dressing.

Approaching Keira was a risky move but one I was willing to take. Although I had apprehension about the case and the possibility of innocent people being at risk, my adrenaline pumped hard and heavy.

Ainsley told us Keira and Bellamy ate lunch here every day at 12:30. I hoped his intel was correct. At 12:15, the girl delivered my salad without saying a word. I should have tried the cheeseburger joke to make sure she was alive. I picked at the salad to kill time and after a long fifteen minutes, my phone chirped. *"They are here."*

Bellamy and Keira came into the restaurant and took a table near the front. The same waitress went to their table with two glasses of sparkling water and did say hello to them. *I guess there were advantages to being regulars.* I laid a pen recorder on my table and aimed it toward them. I clicked the record button, but did not expect much. Two other couples were at tables and the pen would pick up all the extraneous conversations and noise.

A tall girl with short brown hair came in and stood in the doorway for a moment, scanning the restaurant, then announced, "Does anyone drive a Range Rover?"

Bellamy perked up. "I do."

The girl went to his table, said something, and Bellamy got up, threw his napkin on the table and followed her out. I laid some bills on my table to cover the salad, put the pen in my pocket, and then went to Bellamy's table and slid into his seat.

Keira Kaine's blue eyes went wide. "Excuse—"

"Ms. Kaine, please don't say a word. My name is Rhodes. You do not know me, but I know you. I have a business proposal for you, and you only. Meet me tonight at eleven at Club Cuba. I will be at the end of the bar wearing a black ball cap." I stood. She began to speak but I interrupted. "Club Cuba. Eleven. Make sure you're alone."

I made a quick exit and passed Bellamy as he came back in. I scurried one block, turned right, and hopped into the backseat of the waiting Taurus. Quade pulled the car into the street.

"Well?" Katie said.

"You were perfect. Now take off the wig before someone sees you."

"You think she'll show?" Quade asked.

"Definitely."

25

"Didn't show up?" Mike asked, as he dealt out—thank God—cheeseburgers and fries. I needed immediate corrective action on the salad from Lulu's.

"No, I waited an hour, sent messages to the phone. Nothing."

The three of us had convened in my condo to discuss the now missing George Ainsley, and the pending meeting with Keira Kaine. Quade had files spread out on the kitchen table while Katie fumed downstairs in McNally's. Someone had to work.

"We verified he did not go to work?"

"Yes. Did not answer his desk phone or cell phone, and we cannot get close enough to the building to search for his car. He did not meet me this morning, no call, no answer at his apartment, and as far as we can tell, did not go to work."

"Can we get in his apartment?"

I pulled the platter of fires in front of me. "You and I can. I doubt Special Agent Quade would object."

Quade put down his pen and took a draw on his beer. "I don't want to ask for a warrant to enter his apartment because that will raise questions and I want this as quiet as possible. If our blonde friend got wind he was working against her, or happened to hire a private investigator, she has motive to send her flunkies to remove him from the equation. Now, if you two happen to wander by..."

"Nothing we can't handle." Mike nodded to me, and then focused on Quade. "Tell me again about the Russian connection."

Quade held up a picture of the tall, skinny Russian. "First, facial recognition came back confirming this one to be Maxim Vlasova. The second guy came back with a possible ID—name of Makarov. Nothing conclusive, though."

He pulled up a file on his computer and opened a picture of Keira sitting at a table at an outside café, plus dozens of other photos of her out in public, shopping, walking on a city street, and standing in line at a bank. "She came on our radar five years ago, I was new out of the academy and assigned to New York. The Russians were doing a lot of business in the city and we had an angle on a couple of players. They operated from behind an import company—I know, cliché, these guys were never ultra-smart, just ruthless—and controlled much of the action on the docks. Drugs held the most profit, and they constantly battled the cartels for their slice."

"Cartels reach to New York?" Mike asked.

"Been retired awhile, I guess." Mike raised an eyebrow and Quade got the message. "They reach all over the world. The cartels have more money, more guns, the best electronics, cars, planes, you name it, and no problem getting drugs across the border and selling. The problem is what to do with the cash."

"Launder?"

"Yep. I'm a rookie agent and I got the grunt work. Which meant following and photographing a married couple who would launder money for the Sinaloa cartel. The Delgados, Alberto and Carletta. They would make their rounds through New York, collecting cash from drug wholesalers, and then make small deposits, less than ten thousand—"

"To keep it from being reported," I said.

"Right, in eight different banks in Manhattan. Did this for years. You could set your watch by them."

"Why didn't you move in?"

"We were building a case against the wholesalers, suppliers, runners, and wanted to follow it backward to intercept the drugs coming into the city. But, politics ruined the fun. When there is that much cash being tossed around, someone is always looking the other way, and nothing happens. Everyone is on the payroll.

"Anyhow, one day we are following the Delgados and they meet a Russian, Dmitry Orlov—no stranger to us. The Russians and Mexicans never play nice, so we thought that was interesting. I make Orlov my priority. Turns out he worked a side deal with the Delgados to hustle cash for him. They would meet at a coffee shop on West Fifty-Fourth Street every Wednesday morning at nine.

"The arrangement goes on for about four months when, low and behold, one fine spring day in New York City, Orlov does not show up to deliver the cash, but this tall blonde supermodel walks into the shop and drops a package at the feet of Alberto. The same thing happens the following week and we have no idea who she is. Some babe recruited by Orlov. We put a tag on her and find out her name is Keira Kaine. Had a Long Island address, studied engineering on a scholarship at Fordham, and now a money runner for Orlov? I'm sure Orlov paid well, but something about it did not fit."

"Got to trust your gut," I said.

"Yes, exactly. My gut told me to keep looking and two weeks later, she disappears. Dropped out of sight, never to be heard from again. Until six weeks ago."

"Yeah?"

"The NSA picks up chatter between the Washington rezidentura and some woman in Port City unknown to them. Around the same time, the Department of Defense receives a report detailing inappropriate behavior by the owner of Bellamy Space Technologies. Keira Kaine's name pops up and we confirm she's been working there for about two years."

"George Ainsley sent the report?" I asked.

"Yep, and here I am."

"Our research had her going to college at Cal State Fullerton."

"Yes, after Fordham and her time with Orlov, she went to California and into the aerospace industry, then batted her eyes at Bellamy."

Mike got up and came back with a round of beers. "Why was she working the money laundering and why do I think another shoe is about to land?"

Quade opened his beer and toasted Mike. "My theory is the laundering gig was part of her tradecraft training. My bigger theory is she is a sleeper."

"Sleeper agent?" I asked.

"We can't confirm her existence in this country before Fordham. There are no records of her going to elementary or high school on Long Island or anywhere in the US."

"You think they brought her into this country for the purpose of infiltrating Bellamy?"

"Yes, Bellamy and Ainsley made their breakthrough on the solar power thing four years ago. So the timing is right, plus she's the perfect package, with the education and looks."

"Talk about a playing the long game," I said.

"Long game times ten. However if she pulls it off, well worth it. The Russians would love a peek at those plans."

"Pick her up."

"For what? She didn't do anything illegal—yet. I want to wait and nail her on espionage and lock her away. But, the pussies in our government will send her back to Moscow with a slap on the wrist. Enough of my commentary."

"Let move on to tonight," I said.

"Stick to the plan. Gauge her reaction. Let her make the next move."

"She might run."

Mike grabbed a handful of fries. "Not with your charming personality."

***

Mike and I drove to Ainsley's place and found what we expected. Nothing. It was a small one-bedroom garden apartment and it took Mike less than thirty seconds to jimmy the lock. The living area was neat and tidy with a sofa, television, and one wall lined with bookshelves. He had a laptop on a computer stand and on a small sideboard table sat a bottle of Macallan 12 and one glass.

"Decent taste in Scotch," Mike said.

We checked through the kitchen and bedroom and found more of the same. Clothes hung in a walk-in closet, all coordinated by color. The top of his dresser was bare and he only had a lamp on a nightstand. Not one picture in the place. No family photos, landscapes, nothing.

"Jackpot," Mike said. Engineering manuals and books on history, government, and politics jammed the bookshelves, except for Mike's discovery. "I think this is a complete collection of every *Playboy* magazine ever published." Each one was encased in a plastic sleeve.

"Wow. Is the first one there, the one with Marilyn Monroe?"

He pulled one from the shelf and started to open the plastic. "Yup."

"Don't do it. You might rip a page."

"You're right. Hate to ruin the collection by stealing a centerfold."

"A smart, simple man who enjoyed Scotch whiskey and pictures of naked girls. Nothing wrong with that."

"Nope." Mike picked out random copies and examined the front covers. "Just disappeared, huh?"

"As far as we know."

"File a missing persons?" he asked.

"The niece has to. She's next of kin."

"No sign of foul play?"

"No."

He tucked a magazine back in its place on the shelf. "Imagine that."

Sometimes having a person in your life who can read your mind and finish your sentences is a blessing, and sometimes that person can be damn infuriating.

26

Leah Love was the mastermind behind Club Cuba. She was also the woman I fell in love with on the day I arrested her for operating a high-end escort service. She beat the rap in record time and we maintained a cozy relationship ever since. It was not an everyday deal, but a comfortable knowledge we were there for each other. She had a life running her business, and I had mine and one day in the future, the two would merge.

She carried an Ivy League education, an off-the-charts I.Q., and a talent for turning ideas into gold. She immigrated to the States from a Caribbean island and worked on Wall Street for a few years before succumbing to her entrepreneurial spirit. After the escort service closed, and it only folded because of an argument with one of her female escorts who blew the whistle—what is the saying, women are smarter than men, but they can't get along?—she launched herself into the restaurant business with the spice and flair of a seasoned restauranteur.

Club Cuba was her latest creation and it was the place to see or be seen. Live music five nights a week, a four-star menu, and a bar scene that bucked the trendy joints and stayed hot and fashionable, and all with an Afro-Cuban vibe. Any other person would be satisfied with her dose of success, but Leah had to keep moving, scheming, and dreaming. She was a restless soul and I understood years would pass before she would want to settle with me.

She concocted a lucrative side business employing a stable of "strong arms," as she called them—all former Army Rangers, turned mercenaries, turned security experts. Most of the jobs they take were personal protection assignments for high net worth individuals: foreign travel coordination, security consulting, site safety assessments, and surveillance. They also kept an eye on the club when not on assignment. Leah could supply help for almost any predicament or situation— legal, lethal, or otherwise. Example: Emmanuel Blackmon worked for Leah and she owned the beach safe house.

She went out of her way to assist desperate people with nowhere to turn, and when the police come up short and run out of options, someone always knows someone and the path eventually led to Leah. I always thought it was her rebuke of law enforcement to reach across the line and pull someone from the abyss when proper channels failed. Her only rule was to help innocent people who were victims in situations beyond their control.

She and her team were up to speed with Keira Kaine. I took my place at the end of the Club Cuba bar, exchanged a glance with Leah from across the room, but she would not dare talk to me. She had tradecraft wired in since birth.

She looked like a million dollars from the moment she put a foot on the floor in the morning to when she locked the door at night. Tonight she was stunning in a white, sleeveless, knee-length dress that hugged the curves like an Indy car at two hundred miles per hour. Her hair long, black and silky, and her dark eyes were deep pools that reached out and sucked me under every time. Her caramel skin contrasted with the backless white dress and defied any man not to sneak a second peek.

She greeted guests and kept a sharp eye on every facet of the restaurant. She knew what happened at every moment in her establishment, and all with a smile any Hollywood actress would sell their mother to have.

Ten minutes after I sat at the bar, she walked behind me and traced a finger along my back as she passed, which told me her men were in place with eyes around the building, inside and out. Julio was her bartender and I ordered a bourbon with ice.

Julio came back with my drink. "Going to be busy tonight."

That meant Keira was here and not alone. We all worked on the assumption she had people positioned in the restaurant. Midway along the bar, to my right, an African American couple were having drinks, at the opposite end of the bar sat an older man sipping a martini, and a table in the dining room had two men eating dinner.

I motioned for Julio and he came to me. I pushed a twenty across the bar for no other reason but to stay in character. "White paneled van with two Caucasian males?"

He nodded. "Need change?"

"Keep it." I sent a quick text: *"White van."*

Eleven fifteen came and went and as I began to wonder whether she would show, the older man at the end of the bar created a bit of commotion by lighting a cigarette. Julio threw his bar rag down and went to remind the man he could not smoke in the restaurant. The band was on a break so everyone at the bar heard the dust-up, and then the man got up, flicked the cigarette into his martini and hurried out.

The disturbance over, I turned back to my drink, only to find Keira Kaine standing beside me.

Well executed diversion. I never saw her come in.

"I was beginning to think you stood me up."

She wore jeans, boots, a white T-shirt, and black blazer. She took the stool next to me and angled to face me. Julio came over and she ordered vodka on the rocks. "I'm here and you have five minutes." She was striking, with a long face and the high cheekbones of her supermodel persona, but she had dark-blue eyes, almost violet, that penetrated as she talked. Not the warm, sparkling blue of Katie's eyes; these were cold and almost lifeless, but I could see why Bellamy, or any other man, would be entranced.

All I thought of was the stunner in her flunkie's gut.

"Fair enough. Thank you for coming," I said. "My name is Rhodes and I will not waste your time. You impressed my employers with your work at Bellamy Space and they would love to talk to you. Through me."

"About?"

I smiled. "Working for them."

"Not interested."

"Can I elaborate?"

She did not blink. "Doesn't matter. We are not interested in any type of merger or joint venture. We've been approached before and do not need a partner."

"The deal is for you—only you. You will make ten times the money you and your boyfriend Bellamy will make."

"You do not know what you're talking about."

"The advancements you engineered in the space-based solar program are highly anticipated."

"Who is your employer?"

"The problem is you made a mess with your involvement with Bellamy. The wife is quite unhappy. A woman scorned and all."

"Nothing to do with my work."

"Until she files for divorce and takes half the company."

Julio served her vodka and she took a sip. "Who is your employer?"

I smiled. "In due time."

"Our meeting is over."

"Miss Kaine, do you think the government is going to allow you and Bellamy to sit back and collect fat checks? They might sing your praises, but they will claim the technology as their own. Between Mary Ann Bellamy and the US government, I say you consider my offer."

"Which is?"

"Eight figure deal for starters, as long as you bring the technology with you."

"Impossible."

"Anything is possible." I slid her a business card. "Call me at this number. I'm sure we'll meet again." She picked up the card. "Such a shame about Mary Ann Bellamy and her accident. I'm glad she's okay. Funny when you think about it. It would have solved a problem for you."

She stood, studied me for a moment, tucked the card into her jeans pocket, turned and walked out through the front of the restaurant.

Mission accomplished. I stayed at the bar and had Julio pour me another. "Hot," he said, "but got a weird vibe. Like she's evil or something."

"You don't know how right you are, my friend."

I waited until I received a text telling me the white van had drove off. I went out through the back to my Buick parked in the alley. Headlights at the end of the alley flashed twice, the all clear sign from Leah's men.

***

Leah lived in the oceanfront penthouse condominium high atop the Atlantic Shores building, ten miles south of the city. She had a five-year-old Super Tuscan opened and waiting, along with a plate of meats, cheeses, and breads. Light jazz music filled the rooms because she knew what soothed my soul. We took the wine and antipasto to the balcony and stretched out on lounge chairs. We toasted a good night's work, how well we are together, and I kissed her under a sky full of stars. We brought each other up to date on the latest in our lives, the future, and discussed how content we were with the current version of our relationship.

A cool breeze blew in from the ocean so we moved inside. I poured us each another glass of wine.

Then I slowly unzipped her dress.

27

The morning sun peeked over the Atlantic and bathed the bedroom in gold. I sat on the edge of the bed, contemplating the day ahead while soaking in the sunrise and all its wonder.

Leah stirred. "Hey."

I turned to her. She was naked under the sheet, so I did what any red-blooded boy would do. I pulled the sheet off, slowly, inch by inch, until I revealed all her sensual splendor. Beauty was in the eye of the beholder and to this beholder, the warm glow of her caramel skin against the white sheets was too much too resist. I laid back and pulled the sheet over us.

An hour later, we brought pastries and coffee to the balcony and sat in the chairs as the day warmed. "This should be our life every morning," I said.

"It will be."

I sipped the black coffee and enjoyed the sun, the moment, and Leah. She was curled up in a white terry cloth robe. Her dark eyes sparkled in the morning light, silky black hair fell around her face, and it was a vision I wished I could capture forever.

Instead of enjoying the moment, I ruined it with talk about work. "Any idea how she got into the club?"

She shook her head. "It bothers me, too. We gave the security video to the FBI. Julio sent over the glass she used in case you need fingerprints, and the guys did stick a tracker on the van."

"You didn't tell me last night?"

"We were preoccupied."

I grabbed her hand and kissed it. "Thank you."

"Which part?" she said with her cute, coy smile.

"All parts. The club and here. But, there was that one little thing you did, I can't quite figure out how—"

She stood, took the coffee cup from me, grabbed my hand, and led me back inside to the bedroom.

"Leah, you're stuck with me, you know."

"And you are stuck with me."

***

They were in a line in the back of the bar with arms folded across their chests. Mike, Katie, and Quade, ready to hold an inquisition.

I stopped. "What?"

"Now you're James Bond? Make contact with a spy, and then bed down a beautiful woman," Mike scolded. "We all waited for you."

"You're jealous."

The door opened and a couple came in.

"Oh brother, testosterone level is rising. Saved by the customers." Katie left to wait on them.

The three of us slid into the booth. "Sorry, something came up at the last minute." They sat across from me and stared, waiting for an explanation as if I were a teenager who stayed out all night without permission. "I said I was sorry."

"I hoped to debrief, last night," Quade said.

"It went as well as expected. She had people in the club. Did you identify the man with the cigarette?"

"We sent the footage from the club's security camera. No name, but the Washington field office confirms him as a Russian embassy employee. No doubt a low-level operative."

"Bad mistake on her part if he links back to the embassy. Say good-bye to the defense contract," Mike said.

"No kidding." I handed Quade a bag I had brought in. "The glass she used, plus we got a tag on the van. So, how did she sneak past us?"

"Only thing I can figure—she was in there early, in disguise." Quade tapped the bag. "This is perfect. God knows what her fingerprints will reveal, if anything."

"Still can't believe we missed her."

Quade opened his computer and cued up the club security footage. "We've gone through this three times so far. There was a woman, with short brown hair and glasses, sitting with a man at a table in the front of the club. The woman appeared to have the same body type as Keira, and wore the same white T-shirt. Could be her. Not sure about the man. Middle-aged, white, stocky. Facial recognition returned nothing." He scrolled through the video and stopped on the image of the couple at the table. "Right here, they get up and leave, and if the time is correct, it's when your man lights his cigarette."

The time code had 11:17:42. "The time is dead on. I remember checking my watch at 11:15 and it was a few minutes later when he lit up." He pressed play and the camera showed them putting money on the table. The man walked out of frame toward the entrance; she slung an oversized purse on her shoulder and moved off in the opposite direction. "Wearing jeans; could be her. She made a quick change in the ladies' room and then met me at the bar, but she didn't have a purse with her."

"You're right. No purse when she left. Means she had help in the bathroom. Doesn't matter anyhow. If it was her, it proves her access to assets and resources," Quade surmised.

Katie set three mugs of draft beer in front of us. Mike and I grabbed ours and gulped them down.

Quade looked like a six-year-old who dropped his ice cream cone. "I'm on duty."

Mike rolled his eyes. "We're all family here. No cameras in this place."

"You sure?"

Mike pushed the beer to him.

Eagle Scout Quade hesitated, then hoisted the mug and chugged it down like a frat boy on a dare. He slammed the mug. "Damn, sometimes there's nothing better than a cold beer."

Mike got up and collected the mugs. "Like a potato chip, you can't have just one." He refilled them, came back, and we all dove in again.

"Now, moving forward?" Mike asked.

"We wait for her to contact me," I said. "If I don't hear anything within one day, I'll make a second contact."

"I agree," Quade said. "And I want eyes and ears in the motel where the two Russians are staying. Job for Eric and Ortiz."

"Hold up," Mike said, with steel in his voice, and never one to mince words. "Keira is a high-level executive at a defense contractor, working on a top-secret solar-powered something or other, and she's having an affair with Bellamy, the owner of the company. Bellamy's wife was run off the road, and poor old man Ainsley, who is now missing, thinks she is angling for all the glory. On top of all that, the FBI is scared she's going to fly back to the motherland with the secrets."

"Plus she has a stun gun and is not afraid to use it," I said.

Quade leaned back in the booth. "You summed it up."

"And, Johnny, why were *you* hired?" Mike asked, his point not lost on us. "What exactly are we doing?"

Quade's turn to talk. "Guys, you said it yourselves. She'll sniff out the FBI from miles away. I appreciate what you've done, but if you can see this through with me—another day or so? We confirmed Bratva is working with her, and the guy in the club last night was probably FSB, which is Russian counterintelligence."

"We know what FSB is," Mike said.

"Right. Anyhow, best-case scenario, we catch her plotting against the government. Worst case, she runs and at least we've foiled her plot."

"Worst case?" Mike's Irish face turned red. "Ainsley is gone. Forget about him?" He got up and went to the kitchen.

Quade called after him. "Mike, of course not." He sat back and ran his hand over his head, and then finished off the last swallow of his beer.

"Don't worry, young stud. I will finish what we started," I said. "Nevertheless, Mike is right. We didn't sign on for this, and he's seen too many best-laid plans go sideways many times. Now we have a man missing."

"Johnny, I understand—"

"Here's the deal. I'm in, but the second I sense something, or see, or touch, or smell something I don't like, I pull out and take my people with me. We are dishing out a lot of goodwill for the government here, but my loyalties are to protect my client."

"Copy that."

28

Emmanuel met me as I pulled into the safe house driveway. I got out of the car and he walked with me up the stairs that led to the front deck and entrance. "How's our guests?"

"Making themselves at home. Mrs. Bellamy keeps to herself, subdued. Pleasant enough. The other one, Brynne, is wearing out a path from the bar to the deck. She stays juiced."

"Is that a bad thing?"

"Nope. Walks around in a bikini all day. No complaints from me or Jamal. She's hot and loves to flaunt it," he said.

"Just make sure she's sober in case you need to make a quick exit. I don't anticipate any trouble, but our adversary has much more extensive resources than we first believed. Stay on your toes."

"Ten-four on that."

"Our new arrival?"

"Can't tell you too much. Stays cooped up in the study reading and drinking Scotch. You sent me some lushes."

"Sorry. Let's hope it's only a few more days and then you're off to something more exciting than babysitting."

"No problem, boss. Diversion like this I don't mind."

"How about our other business?"

"Happening today."

"Excellent."

I went in to the great room of the house and it was empty. Emmanuel was correct; they did make themselves at home. A pair of sandals was on the floor, bath towels hung off the back of the sofa, magazines and breakfast plates and cups littered a coffee table, and the television blared some nonsense. The kitchen, not any better. Trash overflowed the can, dishes filled the sink, two empty vodka bottles on the counter, and a pot on the stove with leftover spaghetti and tomato sauce in it. The two country clubbers from affluent, upper-class homes turned into college freshman co-eds within two days. If Leah walked in right now, these two would find themselves in a Motel Six faster than you could say housekeeping.

I slid open the deck door and found Mary Ann and Brynne stretched out on lounge chairs soaking up the sun. Mary Ann wore capri pants and a T-shirt. Brynne, ever the more daring, had on yellow bikini top and skimpy pair of shorts. Music pumped from a radio. They each had a drink beside them on a table, and both had their faces in a magazine.

"If I was the killer, you two would be done," I said. They jumped. "I see it has been a real hardship for the two of you to stay here."

"Are you kidding? I'm not leaving." Brynne was off the chair and threw her arms around me. "We wondered when you would be back."

"Seem to be doing fine without me."

Mary Ann turned down the music and stood. "Hi, Johnny." She extended her hand and I shook it. "Any news? You surprised me yesterday."

"How are you feeling?"

"Still sore, but improving. Relaxing here is what I needed."

"Good. Let's go in and talk."

Brynne followed us inside until I reminded her Mary Ann was my client and I could only speak with her.

"Well, can I least make you a drink?" Brynne asked.

"Sure, thanks." Mary Ann and I settled at a small dining table off the kitchen. "First, are you comfortable here in the luxurious beach shack?"

"Of course we are, Johnny. The place is marvelous. We love it, but I want to go home. I hope you have information for me."

"I do not yet have the proof you want—the reason you hired me—but the investigation into Keira, and your husband, raised a few other questions," I said.

"Oh?"

"Did you have much interaction with Keira? Ever get to know her at all?"

She shrugged. "No. Tom and I have—had—a Christmas party every year. She came last year, mostly stayed to herself, hung by Uncle George most of the evening."

"She come alone?"

"Yes. Then left early. I remember because the rest of the women all talked about her. Nobody liked her. Except for Tom, I guess. The affair had begun at that point and I was the naïve wife who didn't have a clue. The others tried to ignore the awkwardness—and arrogance—of her being in my house."

"What about her personal life?"

"All I know is what you already know. She was working for a firm in California and met Tom and my uncle at a conference. They raved about her taking the job at BST and I never thought anything more until Uncle George complained about her." Brynne came with one of her gin and tonic specialties. "She can stay. Brynne knows everything anyhow."

Brynne stopped behind my chair and massaged my shoulders. "Tense...muscles are tight. You could use a deep tissue massage."

"Between the drink, the massage, and the bikini, I'm losing my focus."

"Maybe you should aim your focus in a different direction?" Mary Ann laughed and Brynne gave me a hug from behind. "You two get back to work. I'm on the deck."

"She always like that?" I asked.

Mary Ann shook her head. "Enjoying her new-found freedom."

I sipped the drink. I don't know what she did different, but she sure could mix a gin and tonic. "You and your uncle drive the same car."

"Yes. He admired mine so much, he bought himself..." It took her a moment before she figured it. "Oh, God. They thought I was him."

"Yep."

"Dear Jesus. You think she wanted to kill him?"

"The three of you need to stay in this house until I tell you."

"You're scaring me."

"The house is the safest place for you. Emmanuel and his guys are the best."

George Ainsley was asleep in a cozy, brown leather recliner in the study. The room had a mahogany writing desk, floor-to-ceiling bookshelves lined with Leah's extensive library of classics, plus a pricey collection of first editions. Ainsley had a copy of le Carrè's, *The Spy Who Came in from the Cold* open in his lap. A half-empty bottle of Scotch and a glass were ready and waiting on the desk.

I reached back and knocked on the door.

His eyes opened and it took him a second to clear the cobwebs.

"Mr. Delarosa."

"Impressive collection, isn't it."

"Yes. I could stay here forever," he said.

"Me too." *Only for different reasons.*

"Any updates? I still refuse to believe I was a target." He was now awake and remembering why I brought him here. "She and I...she and I worked well together."

"Maybe so, George. However, there are reasons to believe her motives are more than the accolades and a fat payday."

"How so?"

"The feds confirm evidence connecting her to a foreign government."

He stared at me for a second, and then held up the novel. "You been reading too many of these. She is a razor-sharp engineer with an extremely lucrative future in this industry." He got off the chair, poured himself a Scotch and offered me one that I shook off. "Whomever our landlord is sure has excellent taste in liquor."

"The FBI was tipped by your complaint. You put her name in front of them."

"*She* was not my complaint. Tom allowed himself to be distracted. We are showing weakness at the top and that opens the door for competitors."

"How so?" I asked, but Ainsley's concern was perfect for my Arthur Rhodes cover.

"We are in a business that requires a top-secret level clearance and security. No different from a senator being seduced out of a government secret. Any fissure in our foundation, any sign of dysfunction within the company, and the enemy will pounce. A little gossip goes a long way and the owner of the company having an affair with a senior executive and causing a divorce would be the perfect opening for the jackals. The world is waiting for our technology and Tom is screwing around."

"You complained you were being cut out of your own project."

"I had to do something. I needed to scare Tom into believing me, and I thought the pressure of a DOD inquiry would jolt him back to reality before BST is seduced right out from under him. Then he and I will both be on the outside looking in."

I left Ainsley sulking in his own stew—and the Scotch—said good-bye to Mary Ann and Brynne, and reassured them their stay at the beach-side paradise would only be another few days at the most. I also reminded them we did not have maid service.

Emmanuel saw me off and I no sooner got fifty yards from the house when my burner phone chirped.

A message from Keira Kaine: *"Can we meet?"*

Right on time Keira. Right on time.

29

A second text came from Keira a moment later. *"7 a.m. Santorini's 10ᵗʰ St. Tomorrow."* I shot back a confirmation, and then sent Quade a message that we were on for the morning.

I parked the BMW in my garage behind McNally's and went in through the kitchen. Mike and Katie were leaning against the bar, staring at the television.

Mike pointed at the screen. "You see this?"

The local evening news was on and a young reporter was on the scene at the harbor docks, where a crane was pulling a white Lexus SUV from the water.

Again, the authorities are saying there was no body found in the car, but they did say the vehicle belongs to a Mr. George Ainsley of Port City. And, according to police, Mr. Ainsley cannot be located at this time. The investigation continues. Back to you in the studio.

Katie grabbed my arm. "Johnny?"

"Unfortunate."

"What do you mean? Is that Mr. Ainsley's car? What happened?"

"I told you he did not show up for breakfast yesterday."

"You think he's dead?"

"I think he's missing, and it just so happens that he and Mary Ann Bellamy drive the same car. My money says our Russian friends went after the wrong car. Ainsley was the target all along."

"Oh my God." She plopped down in a booth. "This is terrible. That poor man. He was a little quirky, but didn't deserve this. Are you going to tell Mrs. Bellamy?"

"I already told her."

"And?" She got up and followed me as I went behind the bar and poured myself a bourbon and headed to my booth. "Johnny! What did she say?"

"Sit down and lower your voice."

She slid in opposite me and for the first time I saw an emotion I had not seen in her before—fear. She always had this naïve bravado about her, a happy-go-lucky, afraid-of-nothing, we-can-conquer-the-world attitude. This was different. The Ainsley business affected her.

"Trust me. You know this case is more than following Bellamy and his girlfriend. I need to keep you from view."

"Whose view?"

"You witnessed Keira in action. If the Russians associate you with me, they'd snatch you up in a Moscow minute. Gives them plenty of leverage."

She sat back in the booth. "You think they killed Mr. Ainsley?"

"We'll find out." I leaned across the table to lower my voice and to also emphasize my point. "We've talked about this before. This is real life. These people are ruthless and to them, Ainsley is nothing but a small nuisance. A fly to be swatted to the ground. They won't give a second thought to eliminating him. You either."

She didn't respond but sat with wet eyes and arms folded across her chest.

"Keep doing what you are doing with the trackers on the computer. That is critical. We need to know where they are at all times. Bellamy, Keira, the goons. I am meeting Keira tomorrow morning at seven. Restaurant called Santorini's."

"Make sure you still have the small GPS button Scott gave you." She got up and went behind the bar.

***

Four cars and the white van were the only vehicles in the lot of the no-tell, rent-by-the-hour Starry Night Motel when I arrived at nine. I pulled around to the back of the two-story building and took another look at the text message I received from Eric. He and Ortiz had set up in Room 214, one floor above and one room over from the two Russians in Room 112. I made my way up the back stairs to the second floor and Agent Ortiz opened the door when I knocked.

"PI Dude!" The room had two full-size beds, cheap brown paneling on the walls, matted and worn orange shag carpeting, a small television bolted to a scuffed-up dresser, and the place reeked of sweat, stale beer, and cigarettes. Eric sat on a bed with two laptops open on a table he had pulled close. "Welcome to the seventies."

"Has it been cleaned since the seventies? Is it safe to sit down?"

"At your own risk." Ortiz moved some files off the bed to clear a spot for me beside Eric. "Don't even think about using the bathroom."

I sat down and sunk a good six inches. "Let's not stay here any longer than we need. How did you do?"

"You forget you are in the presence of a mad genius," Eric announced. "I have audio in their room but we didn't have time to get a camera in. Katie sent an alert that their van was heading back. We had to scram."

"This dude is a genius. Somehow he turned his key card into a master key."

"They really need a firewall. Took me less than two minutes once I logged on their network. They have Wi-Fi but can't clean the bathrooms."

"Could you see how they paid for the rooms?" I asked.

"Cash."

The special agent stretched out on the other bed. "They are both in the room but their conversations are in Russian. Only the TV for the last hour, though."

Eric turned up the volume on a small speaker attached to the receiver and it was the drone of a soccer match. "How far will the bug transmit? Because this mad genius is hungry and I'd much rather listen from the car instead of this rat hole."

"Hundred yards without any obstruction. I can stay if you two want to make a food run."

"Groovy, PI Dude. Why are we listening to these two, anyhow?"

"Anything that will clue us into—"

A noise from the Russians' room came over the speaker.

"Was that a knock on their door?" Ortiz jumped up and we huddled around.

Their voices went back and forth, and then one of the Russians opened the door.

"Hey." A female voice. The door closed. "Wait, you didn't say it was two of you."

"It okay. We pay for two." A male voice, in broken English. "Here, here."

"No way. Gonna be forty each."

"Okay, okay, we pay."

"One at a time."

"Yes."

"Damn, they hired a hooker," Eric said. "Oh, shit, we are down and in it."

Ortiz and I traded a glance. She was probably as amused and confused by the Eric speak as I was. The speaker went silent. Thirty seconds later we heard a rustling around and bed squeaks.

A long, deep moan..."Baby, baby."

"This is awkward," Ortiz said.

One final grunt, and then laughter, from the other man. One man yelling and one laughing.

"That was quick." The female voice.

The Russian voices argued back and forth until a door slammed.

"Did he leave?" I asked.

Ortiz peeked through the drapes. "No. Maybe he's so humiliated he hid in the bathroom."

Eric flopped back on the bed. "The dude is a minute man. It's okay dude. We've all been there."

"Yeah?" Ortiz asked.

Eric's face turned red, and I was about to add a witty tidbit to the conversation, when all three of our phones buzzed.

A text from Katie: *"Keira's car approaching."*

Eric popped up. "No way. Dude, this will be off the chain."

I sent a message back: *"How far?"*

"One mile."

"Katie, good job."

Ortiz stayed at the window. Moans and grunts came through the speaker. We surmised it was now the second Russian's turn. I had a tiny bit of sympathy for these two because when the blonde walked through the door, their time serving the motherland could come to a painful halt.

"She's here." Ortiz closed the gap in the drapes.

Keira must have a key because the door opened without a knock and the screaming began immediately. Mostly in Russian but we heard enough English to figure what was happening.

"Screwing a whore with my money...get out...now..."

The door slammed. Ortiz ran to the drapes. "Didn't know hookers could run that fast."

More screaming. "Damn," Eric said, "she's laying them dudes out."

Somewhere in the midst of the screaming, we did hear:

Santorini...

More screaming, then, what I feared:

Nyet... nyet...Nadia...nyet...nyet

"Did he just say her name?" I asked.

"Nadia, he said. Nadia." Ortiz scribbled it in a notebook. A guttural scream came from the speaker followed by a moment of silence.

More rustling around, bed squeaks, a crash...maybe a lamp falling.

Nadia...nyet...sorry, sorry. A second loud cry...

"PI Dude, what is happening?"

"She carries a stun gun."

"Dude, no way. She stunned them?"

"Serious?" Ortiz said.

"Yep."

The door slammed in their room and Ortiz went to the window. "There she goes. Stun gun, huh? Brutal. One way to keep her employees in line."

"I hope her mood lightens because I'm the guy who is meeting her at seven tomorrow morning."

For once, Eric was speechless.

30

Santorini's was a Greek breakfast and lunch hole-in-the-wall, but as luck would have it, I had never been in the place. The danger of donning the Arthur Rhodes persona was taking the chance of being recognized, and even though Keira chose this location, it worked. The Greek section of the city was never my beat as a uniformed cop, and I never had much action in this part of town as a detective. The Greeks kept to themselves, centered their lives around the Orthodox Church, and did a decent job of staying out of trouble.

The warm aroma of fresh brewed coffee hit me as I walked in, and to my right was a pastry case containing some of the most decadent-looking baklava this side of Athens. I made a mental note to come back once the Bellamy business was over.

Ten booths lined the left wall and Keira was in the last booth, the exact location I would choose. Basic operative tradecraft, whether an agent for a government or a private detective surveilling a subject: the goal was to put the establishment in front of you to observe all who entered. She also had the kitchen door behind her in case of a quick exit.

I approached the booth and she gestured for me to sit.

"Glad you reconsidered, Ms. Kaine." A teenage boy came to the table to take my order. "Coffee, black." Keira had a cup of tea in front of her.

"I'm curious," she said.

I thought I looked sharp in the blue suit I chose for the meeting, but she wore black slacks, an oversized black blazer, a white blouse unbuttoned halfway down her chest, and a man's red and black striped necktie loosely tied around the collar. Direct from the pages of *Vogue*.

"You should be. I made a generous offer."

"Why so secretive? Why not contact me through normal channels?"

"A lot of eyes are on you and Bellamy. If word gets out you're open to offers from rivals, it could create a bidding war for you. Think of my offer as a preemptive strike. Eliminate the competition before the competition realizes you were available. Plus, any emails or calls would be traceable."

She nodded. "I'm content where I am."

The young waiter came back with my coffee. "Would you like anything?" he asked. Keira shook her head.

He moved to the next table. The Greek coffee tasted as good as the aroma advertised. Quade's history of Keira working for the Russian mobster Orlov kept playing in the back of my mind. She sat here in designer clothes from the runways of Milan, blue eyes that could turn a man to mush, looks that should put her in front of a camera, but the black purse on the chair beside her reminded me of her brutality. *Did she carry the stunner with her at all times?*

"Content? Bellamy's divorce will screw it up. Or is that your strategy? Create chaos at the top until the company falls apart? Then swoop in, clean up the pieces, and then reap the rewards? After all, you have all the knowledge and nothing to lose."

"Mr. Rhodes, I'm proud of our work. The last thing I want is to disrupt the organization. If his divorce happens, it's a temporary distraction."

"But here we are."

She shrugged and stirred her tea. "I know the players in this industry, and most cannot afford what you're offering. My time is valuable. Please don't waste it. This offer?"

"You see the news last night?"

"Mr. Ainsley?" She stopped stirring. "Already gave a statement to the police. Had issues, though."

"Yeah?"

"Likes his Scotch. Also could not deal with the fact we were moving from this little R&D company to a player on the main stage. Smart man, spent his career on this technology, then when our breakthrough was apparent, he gets crazy. Resents my involvement, couldn't handle his own success. Starts talking, complaining, and we get scared he's going to blow the whole deal." She took a sip of tea and set the cup down. "Millions at stake and he won't shut up."

I studied her for a moment, hoped to spot a tic, a tell, any sign of nerves. Nothing. She was steely cool. "Is he at the bottom of the harbor?"

She aimed the blue eyes at me. "I need to go to work." She waved for the waiter.

"Do I tell my employers he's a non-issue?" She cocked an eyebrow. "Disgruntled employee found dead. That's heavy baggage," I said.

"Non-issue. I'm sure there's an explanation." The waiter laid the check on the table as he breezed by. She put a five on it. "You have one more minute, but I'll help you along. It's not China—they'll just steal the technology. Japan is too proud to bring in an American, and the Russians are all bluster with no substance. Leaves the private sector. Space X and Centauris are the only two with resources to make that kind of offer. Am I close?"

"More of a private consortium with a goal of providing energy to the world. The project will be all yours. My task is to put you in the room with the CEO, then you never see me again. Can I tell them you agree to meet?"

"Where is the job located?"

"Southwest US. Includes a house and a car. You'll need to supply proof of the technology and that you can deliver."

"How do I do that?"

"Figure it out. You have twenty-four hours."

She sat for a minute staring at me, trance-like. I kept reminding myself that the first one to talk loses.

Finally, she stood and pulled her purse on her shoulder. "Try the baklava." She went out through the front.

"You get all that?" I said.

My cell phone buzzed with a text: *"Yes."* Quade had a microphone/transmitter sewn into the lapel of my suit jacket. He was in a car two blocks from the restaurant and had agents stationed on the side streets.

I bought an order of baklava on my way out.

31

A DO NOT DISTURB sign hung on the door handle of Room 528 of the downtown Hilton. I knocked twice and Eric opened, and judging from the amount of fast-food trash, pizza boxes, and soda cans, he had made himself right at home.

He transformed one of the beds into a command center. He sat against the backboard and on his left was his laptop, situated on a makeshift computer table he fashioned from two folded blankets. To his right was a room service tray, balanced on two pillows, with the TV remote, his phone, and a notepad. On the nightstand was an ice bucket, a glass, and four cans of Mountain Dew.

"Really suffering here, huh?"

"PI Dude, you need to stretch this gig out as far as you can."

"They do have housekeeping."

"Mamacita Ortiz told me to not let anyone in."

The door opened and Quade and Ortiz came in with coffees and a sack of breakfast sandwiches.

"Johnny, stellar work today. I think she's curious if nothing else," said Quade. "She took off the red tie as she walked out of the restaurant."

"Signal?"

"Definitely. From there she went to BST."

"Any sign of her flunkies in the area?"

"No, but that doesn't mean she didn't have people around. What's your gut say?"

I pulled a chair over to the bed and sat. "If your theory is true, and she is FSB, and is intrigued that my deal is legit, she'll contact me to set the meeting. Can't imagine her not wanting a run at one of the bigger players. She holds the cards with Bellamy, but the chance to take the technology to a company with unlimited funds—a more valuable target—might be hard to resist. However, if she sees through me and smells a rat, she tells her handlers and they turn me inside out."

Eric chomped through his egg and cheese sandwich like a chainsaw going through a pine. "What's FSB?"

"Russian CIA. Used to be the KGB."

"If she actually works for them, I think she'll spook and run," Eric said. "Take all the top-secret plans with her."

"Why?"

"Too much drama, dude. She's got to be thinking something is whacked. You, Arthur, shows up just when the divorce shit happens? I mean, your cover—your legend—is solid, but she's sweating. Might not show it, but dude, c'mon." He pointed to my sandwich. "You gonna eat that?" I handed it to him. "What's the ultimate goal, anyhow?"

Quade paced around in a three-foot square. "For her to come to the meeting with a flash drive containing details of their solar energy program, then I nail her on stealing government property and possible espionage charges. Plenty for me to make a case. At the least, she's sent back to Moscow."

"Eric's got a point. I wouldn't do it if I was her." We all turned to Ortiz. This was the first time she offered an opinion since we met. "Even if she is embedded like you think, my money says she'll want proof. She's not taking the risk of divulging the technology without Johnny—Arthur—dropping his pants first. Proof of funds. I know I would. Eric's right—they could pull her and she's on the next plane to sunny Moscow with the goods."

Nobody said anything. Quade opened a sandwich and finished it in two bites, but the last thing I wanted to do was eat. The pit of my stomach told me Ortiz was correct. Keira was not stupid and maybe this entire plan was half-cooked. Mike's concerns banged away in my head. *Are you crazy...you are going to work for them?* Mary Ann hired me to prove the affair, not to jump into international espionage, although, I had to admit, playing secret agent was a gas.

"Maria, you think she'll bail out?" Quade asked.

"Gets too hot, sure," she said. "She screwed up with the affair. The rezidentura can't be pleased at the moment."

"If they know."

"They know. Bellamy is about to announce groundbreaking advancements in this space energy technology, whatever it is, and Moscow has an asset in place right at the top? They are dancing on the tables," Ortiz said. "Until she literally screws herself into the divorce drama. Then Ainsley disappears? They either pull her out or kill her before we even get a chance."

"They won't kill her. They'll want the technology. I say they'll leave her," Quade said.

Agent Maria Ortiz shrugged and sipped her coffee. "No way."

"Anything on the name Nadia?" I asked.

"Our time at the Starry Night paid off. Missing piece of the puzzle." Ortiz took a sheet of paper from an attaché case. "Nadia Ivanovich was an aeronautical engineering student at Moscow Aviation Institute three years before she was spotted in New York, working for Orlov. She completed her degree then disappeared. No records of her in Russia or anywhere in Europe. She first came on our radar when a British asset in Moscow observed her having dinner with a ranking FSB officer. The assumption was she was recruited by FSB, goes through her basic training, gets fluent in English, appears three years later as Keira Kaine at Fordham, and then hones her tradecraft with Orlov."

"After New York, goes to California and works her way into Bellamy," Quade adds.

"Damn, real life spy. Thought that was just in movies," Eric said.

"Nope. Real, dude, and if the heat is turned up like it is now, I think they pull her." Ortiz threw her sandwich wrapper at him. "Real as it gets."

I looked at Quade. "If she calls and wants to meet, who is she meeting with?"

"My ASAC. He'll pose as the company recruiter."

"Dude, I gotta learn these acronyms." Eric's fingers flew over his keyboard. "Assistant Special Agent in Charge?"

"Yep, our boss. And Delarosa," Quade said. "I'll drop by your place later. I think we apply some pressure to Bellamy, make him squirm. Put some doubt in his mind. But I want to talk it through, work up an angle."

"I'll be there. I do have a bar to run."

"Oh, bad news, Eric. The boss pulled the plug on the hotel. Out of funds for this operation. Need to find someplace else for you."

"What? Mamacita, say it's not true."

"Sorry dude. We'll figure something," Ortiz said.

"I'm devastated." He flopped back on the bed. "What about my protection?"

"That won't change."

"You can set up shop at my condo. Okay with you guys?" I asked.

Quade nodded. "Sure. Maria will check on you, and hopefully we will wrap this up in a day or two."

Ortiz packed up her attaché. "Or we can put you up at the Starry Night."

Eric threw the wrapper back at her. "Funny, Mama, funny."

32

We reconvened back at McNally's, and Mike, in a blatant moment of weakness and patriotism, had prepared a lunch of sandwiches and salads for the team and laid it out on a table in the back of the bar.

"My contribution to protecting the secrets of the nation," he said.

"Much appreciated," Agent Ortiz replied, as she helped herself to the spread.

Quade, Ortiz, Mike, and I stood around with plates of food and draft beers and discussed sports, politics, and life in the FBI. Too much small talk for my taste. Katie and Eric came in and made short work of launching into the grub. He was one of those scrawny guys who could eat forever and never gain a pound.

"All set up?" I asked.

"The kitchen table is his new command center and I figured he'll take the sofa. Did Mike make all this?" Katie nodded to the food. "Is he okay?"

"His contribution to the cause."

"We should check his temperature."

I clicked my beer mug on hers. "GPS?"

"Still working, both cars at Bellamy. The white van is at the Starry Night. The potato salad is delicious." She helped herself to another scoop. "What's next?"

"Wait for Keira to contact me."

Eric held up his empty mug. "Another?"

"I need you with a clear head. You are on duty, twenty-four hours a day."

"Damn, dude."

"And if she doesn't?" Katie asked. "Then what?"

"What we were hired to do. Produce evidence of the affair. Which is my objective for tonight."

"I'm going."

"No, I'm asking Mike. I want you and Eric to stay on GPS watch. Keep in contact with me. Our usual."

"Boring, Johnny. I'll bring the laptops, like we did before." She leaned in close to me and whispered. "Don't leave me alone with him. He's weird."

"Eccentric. You can handle him." I handed her some money. "Nothing up there to eat. Lock the boy wonder into the condo and go buy some groceries."

She rolled her eyes. "C'mon, Eric. Now I'm the housekeeper, too."

"I'm not done with my lunch."

"Bring it with you."

Quade and Ortiz were in my booth with the case file open on the table. I sat beside Ortiz. She was not unattractive, more cute than pretty. She never wore makeup and I suspected she was one of those girls who was athletic in school, a high achiever, impressive grades, but her muscular frame masked any sex appeal and that made me wonder whether she hit from the other side of the plate. She could probably drink like one of the boys, too. Either way, her intuitiveness as an agent impressed me, and I would put her on my team any day.

"Unless she contacts me, we're finished," I said. "I did my civic duty. I'm going out tonight to keep an eye on Bellamy. I would love to catch him and our Russian spy together so I can finish my work and get Mrs. Bellamy back home."

Quade nodded. "Fair enough. Any chance you could do us one more favor? Do some recon around her townhouse?"

"The FBI run out of agents? Thought you had a man on the house?"

"We did, but had to send a team to New York because of that last terrorist scare. Only Marie and I on this case and we can't risk it."

"Jesus, Quade. Yeah, sure, Mike and I will check it out."

"Cameras and type of alarm system, if possible. I'm dying to get a look inside the place."

"We'll give it a shot."

"Appreciate it. If she calls, we move forward?"

"Make sure you send me time and place now so I don't stutter when I have her on the phone. I'll take her to the water's edge; from there, it's all you."

"Understood. Thank you. I'll call with a location shortly."

They packed up and went out through the back.

***

Mike rustled up some clothes we used for undercover work we did as detectives and he now wore an old cap and jacket from Charter Cable TV. The jacket had "Bill" embroidered on it. We parked two blocks from Keira's townhouse and he hoofed it to her place, clipboard in hand, first stopping at the neighbors to add credibility to the ruse.

Mike had his Bluetooth in his ear and kept the call open for me to listen. An older, white man opened the door at the townhome next to Keira, and Mike only got as far as, "Hello, sir, my name is Bill from Charter Cable..." when the man slammed the door shut.

"Missed your calling," I said.

"Good thing I didn't do this for a living. Would have locked me up for assault ten times over." He lumbered along the sidewalk to Keira's, checking his clipboard, selling it as best he could. "Camera above the garage door. Now going up the front steps...camera above the door." He knocked. "Draperies are all pulled shut on the windows, can't see anything." He waited a minute then knocked again. No response. "I'm going around back."

An alley ran from the street to the rear of the townhomes, and Keira's home was in the center of the block.

"I am now in the alley. Each house has a deck. She has nothing outside, though. No outdoor furniture, nothing. From the back, you would think her place was vacant. The gate is open...I'm now up the steps to the deck....sliding glass doors...alarm unit confirmed, but a whole lot of nothing, partner."

"Okay, come on back."

"Roger that. On my way. I need a drink."

"I'm buying."

"Hey, wait," Mike said. "One thing. I'm in the alley again and her townhouse is the only one with a satellite dish on the roof."

"So, she hates cable."

"Yeah, but the wires from the dish go into the roof. Don't they usually come down the side of the building then into the house?"

"Got me. Her direct line to Moscow."

"Interesting she's the only one. Makes me think the dish is not for TV."

"Duly noted. Don't push your luck. C'mon back and let's see if we can catch our cheating husband in the act."

"Food first."

"Roger that."

***

We both ate greasy bacon cheeseburgers, fries, and drank draft beers at Joey Mac's, a small corner bar in my old Italian neighborhood owned by an ex-cop, Joe Maccarone. We spent many a day and night in there, even had barstools with our names painted on them. The gregarious Joey had just sat down with us to relive our glory days, when my cell phone chirped.

A text from Eric: *Bellamy on the move.*

"Hate to break up the party, but duty calls. Mike, our man is rolling. Joey, we need to do this later." I pulled some bills from my pocket.

Joey held up his hand. "On the house, boys. Be safe out there."

33

The GPS coordinates placed Bellamy's car at an Econo Lodge in Waterside, a bedroom community ten miles south of Port City, where the harbor opens to the beaches.

"Eyeball his car?" Eric asked, from his new command center in my condo.

I had him on speaker on my cell. Mike was driving his Jeep Wrangler and we were tucked in the back row of the parking lot facing the motel. "Yep. He went into a room on the second floor. Where is she?" I had the camera in my lap. Two or three decent shots of them together fulfills my end of the deal and we put this case to bed. The Keira business is for the feds, anyhow.

"Estimating five miles from you."

"Keep us posted."

"Partner, I need to learn all this GPS stuff. I'm way behind the times," Mike said. "I could never understand this technology if I was out on my own."

"Easy. Do what I do. Ask Katie, or Eric. I should figure a way to hang on to him. His skills are off the charts."

"I heard that," came over my phone's speaker. "Glad you realized how much you need me, PI Dude. Put me on the payroll—you know you want to."

I shook my head while Mike laughed. "Does my phone have a mute button?"

"I'm not telling you now, just as your true feelings are coming out," Eric jabbed. "I told you before I can help you. I am feeling the love, dude. You, me, and dollface will make an awesome team."

"Katie might object to being called dollface," I said.

"She is a dollface. Besides, she'll love it. Women love compliments. I'm diggin' your place here, too. I got the tunes cranked. Thelonious Monk—righteous, man. Hey, this Woodford Reserve whiskey—looks expensive."

"Oh, God," Mike groaned. "Here we go."

"Bourbon, Eric, top shelf bourbon. Put it back and stay out of my liquor cabinet. You're on the job. I need you sharp, not in a drunken haze."

"Chill man. Not my juice anyhow. More of a tequila man. Me and Jose Cuervo are besties."

"You'll grow out of that phase."

"Tequila is for girls. We gotta toughen you up," Mike said, shouting toward the phone. "Teach you to drink like a real man."

"Big Mike, that's harsh. Hey, I'm starving. No food in this crib. I plowed through a box of crackers and your peanut butter. The only thing you got left is microwave popcorn, which I am about to demolish."

"Katie should have been there by now. Call her."

"Copy that. Yo, dude, your girl is close."

"How far?"

"One mile."

"Ending the call. Text me when she is here. Call Katie. Find out where she is." I picked up the camera and focused on Bellamy's room.

"He's entertaining if nothing else." Mike slid his extra-large body lower in the seat and pulled a cap over his red hair.

We lowered the windows in the Jeep and went silent. A minute passed. A text from Eric blinked on my phone: "*Close.*"

The Mercedes parked on the opposite side of the lot from Bellamy's Range Rover. "See that?" Mike said. "Can't get her car and his in the same picture. She's not stupid." She got out and I followed her through the telephoto lens. She climbed to the second floor and tapped on the door with a car key.

"C'mon, Bellamy, open the door and keep it open. I need the two of you in the shot," I said, with an unrealistic optimism.

"The only way to do this is to put a camera in the room," Mike said. "This will be impossible."

He was right. The door cracked opened just enough for her slim body to slide through. I set the camera on the seat. "Shit."

"Now what?" he asked. "They could be shacked up all night."

"Right. Camera inside is what we need. Impossible without knowing where they're going." I called Eric.

"PI Dude, she show up?"

"Yeah, but we couldn't get a picture. Listen—any way to tap his phone? If we knew the location in advance, we could put a camera in."

"Gotta think for a sec...I don't know how to intercept calls, but if we got his phone somehow, I could add a mirror app where we see his text messages in real time. Need the phone, though."

"Do the research; we'll see you back at the condo."

"Copy that, dude."

"Rosswell doesn't have enough?" Mike asked. "Why can't she file for divorce and be on with it? She accused him, and as far as we know, he didn't deny anything."

"Too much money at stake with the company. Jim wants Bellamy balls deep in proof of the affair so he has no choice but to give Mary Ann all she asks for. He screwed himself while screwing the blonde. Sitting on millions with the technology, only to tie it all up in a divorce case. No wonder Ainsley was pissed."

"Speaking of?"

"Tucked away, safe and sound."

"Nice touch with the car in the harbor."

"All meant to spark a reaction but she didn't blink. She didn't kill him so she either believes he did it himself, or Bellamy did it. Or, it's a setup. She probably hopes he offed himself. One less loose end."

Mike started the Jeep but we both saw the room door open. "Hold up," he said. "She's back out."

I grabbed the camera and snapped away. Keira came out of the room, then stopped and turned as Bellamy came out in his trousers and undershirt. She was pointing a finger and yelling; he had his hands on his hips, being scolded like a child. Her voice was not loud enough for us to hear any words, but the picture spoke more than a thousand words. Trouble in paradise.

"You got pictures now, partner," Mike said.

"Sure do. Thank you, Keira." She hurried down the motel steps and into her car and sped out of the lot. I called Eric. "Our girl is on the move. Talk to me."

"Wow, she's flying too. North toward the city."

"Leave the phone open. We'll head that way."

"By the way, PI Dude, your Russian mobster goons must be on vacation. Hanging out on the beach."

"Eric, what did you say?"

"Russians. The white van is at the beach."

"What beach?"

"Not sure. South, past Crescent Beach."

My stomach dropped. "The safe house is compromised."

Oh Jesus, no.

34

It was full dark, no moon to help us. The access road was a one-lane blacktop with sand and sea grass on both sides. The closest house to Leah's beach house was a quarter mile away and it only had a small porch light burning when we went past. We slowed, hoping to come in as silent as possible. I had a thousand questions as to how this house was compromised, but answers would come later. For now, we needed to assess and remedy the situation. On the way down, I sent three 911 messages to Emmanuel. No response.

"Eric?"

He was on speaker on my phone. "The van is still there. Keira's car went off the grid, though. Just stopped blinking."

"She at her house?"

"Nope. In the middle of the city, then poof. Gone."

"Hanging up. Do not call me or Mike. Wait for me to contact you."

"Copy, boss. Hey, be careful."

We crept along, windows down, listening for anything to clue us in to the happenings at the house. The breaking waves off to our left, the occasional croak of a frog, and the hum of the Jeep's engine were the only sounds.

We stopped less than two hundred yards from the house and cut the headlights. Ominous scenarios pinged through my brain. Emmanuel was a smart, intuitive soldier, not one to be caught off guard, so not answering my messages troubled me. He was either without his phone—unlikely—injured, pinned in a dire situation, or worst of all, dead.

"Beulah?"

Mike tapped the roll bar above his head. Beulah was the Remington 700 twelve-gauge shotgun he had his entire police career. The department gave it to him as gift when he retired. He modified the roll bar into a gun case so whenever he drove his vehicle, Beulah was with him. I opened the case and laid the gun across his lap. I gripped my Beretta and clicked off the safety. We both unhooked our seat belts.

"Options?" Mike whispered.

"On the right is a drainage ditch and swamp between here and the main road. The left is sand dunes to go over and then down the beach to the house."

"We're already too close. Bothers me we can't hear anything. No lights on in the house. Voices would carry in the night air."

"Yeah, too quiet."

"I'll take the dune and send you a message when I get to the house," Mike said.

"Copy, partner."

He turned off the Jeep's engine then—*crack!*—the windshield exploded and showered us in a thousand pieces of glass confetti. A second *crack*, and we felt the bullet whiz between us and slam into the back seat with a thud.

"Bail...bail!"

I went out the passenger door in a crouch and dove for the ditch on my side of the road. Mike went out his door and into the high sea grass. Two more shots exploded the quiet night and slammed into the Jeep. A *hiss* and then liquid trickled to the pavement. Hopefully coolant and not gas.

Mike pumped off two blasts into the direction of the house. Ineffective, we were too far away, but it signaled me that he was okay.

"If they have night vison, we are screwed," he yelled.

"I'll give you cover first. Head for the dunes."

I squeezed off three shots to draw them my way and I hoped Mike took advantage. They returned fire as I dove deeper into the weeds, landing in a foot of putrid, stagnant water. The Russians were laying down fire with a high-powered rifle and the first thought through my brain was snakes. Plus, my phone was in my pocket and now under water. *Buck up, Delarosa.*

Silence. Two minutes...three minutes.

I moved from the marsh and crawled closer to the road. Now came the voices. A scream, a woman. *Mary Ann?*

A man's voice, barking orders, yelling. Doors slammed and two lights snapped on; headlights of the van put the Jeep in a spotlight. It also gave me a target. I fired two more shots toward the headlights. No luck.

No time to try my phone. I shouted, "Mike?"

"I'm on it." He must have been on top of the dune.

The van's engine revved and it pulled out, heading our way. At thirty yards, Mike let go a barrage from the shotgun and took out the right headlight. It swerved to its left to miss the Jeep, but caught the right front and spun the Jeep around on the roadway. I emptied my clip into the engine block, but to no avail. The van disappeared into the darkness.

Mike came down from the dune. "Holy shit." His car was demolished. The bumper, glass, plastic, littered the black top.

"You okay?" I asked.

"Yeah. You?"

"Not by a long shot."

Mike retrieved more shells from the Jeep and reloaded the twelve-gauge. I was out of luck, my ammo gone. We took off for the house, heaving and gasping the two hundred yards, adrenaline somehow carried us.

We stopped short of the house and came up as quiet as possible. Two decorative lights at the end of the driveway illuminated a man's body, lying on his stomach. I used my foot to turn him over. Two bullet holes in his chest.

"Keira's man from Club Cuba."

A rustling came from the side of the house. Mike raised the shotgun. "Show yourself." Emmanuel came out of the darkness, dragging one leg, his shirt soaked with blood, his partner, Jamal, draped over his back.

"Johnny, we need help."

35

We laid Jamal on the driveway and tore off his T-shirt. The bullet entered high on the left side of his chest, between his heart and shoulder. Blood pumped freely through the hole and we feared he would bleed out. Mike balled up the shirt and applied pressure.

"Did you call?" I asked.

Emmanuel plopped to the ground and grimaced through clenched teeth. "Yes, they're on their way." He held his hand on his left thigh as blood seeped through his fingers and soaked his pants. He fished a Swiss Army knife out of a side cargo pocket. "Cut my shirt, make a tourniquet."

I did as he said and tied a strip of the cloth around his leg. "Are they gone?"

"My fault...I don't know how....Jesus, this hurts. Johnny, I can't believe we didn't see them."

"How many?"

"At least four, could be more. Maybe a man down in the house. They took Mary Ann and the old guy."

"Brynne?"

He shook his head. "In there, I hope not dead. I'm sorry, Johnny. I'm sorry."

"Not your fault. Keep this tight on your leg. I'm going into the house. Weapon?"

"On the deck."

I went up the back deck stairs, picked up his assault rifle, and entered the great room through the sliding door. No lights on in the house, except for a small one above the sink in the kitchen. "Brynne?" I called. No response.

I thought of turning on a light but did not want to make myself a target in case the other man was still alive. A hallway led from the main room to the first-floor bedrooms, but the first door on the left opened to the library—Ainsley's hangout. I pushed the door with the barrel of the rifle. Too dark. I held the weapon hip high, found the light switch, and clicked it on. The room was pristine, a bottle of Scotch and a glass sitting perfectly on a tray next to his book. No sign of a struggle.

I snapped off the light and went back into the hall. A Maglite on my belt would have been handy at the moment. I made my way to the bedroom on the right and turned on the overhead light. The bed turned down, women's clothes thrown over a wingback chair, and Brynne's duffel bag in the corner.

"Brynne?" Nothing.

Men's clothes hung in the closet of the second bedroom on the first level. Two white shirts and a pair of brown dress pants. A shaving kit sat on the dresser. Ainsley's room. The bed undisturbed, everything neat and tidy. A little too neat and tidy for this late at night. *Why was he not in bed when the attack happened?*

I went back through the center room to the staircase that lead upstairs and found a body spread dead on the steps. One of Keira's crew, but neither of the two Russians from the Starry Night. I stepped over him and slowly went up the stairs to the second floor.

I opened the door to the first bedroom, clicked on the light, and it appeared to be a vacant guest room. "Brynne?" No answer.

Back to the hall and to the next room. I switched on the light. Sheets and blankets were a twisted mess on the bed, and an olive-green army duffel bag with "COLLINGSWORTH" stenciled on the side was in the corner. "Brynne?"

"Johnny?" The voice came from the closet. I pulled the door open and found her curled in a ball on the floor. She saw me, leaped up and threw her arms around me. "Thank God...I thought I was going to die." She wore a tight, white tank top and blue panties. "Never this scared in my life." Her tears flowed, emotions poured out. Between heaves and sobs: "Gunshots...so loud, terrifying...is anyone hurt?"

"Everyone's hurt."

We made our way back to the first floor, stepping over the dead man on the stairs, but she was so distraught, her knees buckled and I practically carried her to her room. "Put on some clothes. Tell me what happened."

"Jamal, is he okay?"

"Shot in the upper chest, ambulance on the way. What happened?"

She pulled on jeans and a sweatshirt. "I...I was in the kitchen and all of a sudden, voices shouting outside then a gunshot. I got scared and ran upstairs and hid in the closet."

"In Jamal's room?"

She hesitated, kept her eyes to the floor when she spoke. "The first room I came to...I just ran." She grabbed a brush and started it through her hair.

I took it from her hand and tossed it across the room.

"No time for that now. Did you see anything? How many guys?"

"I'm not sure...I ran and hid. Johnny, I'm sorry."

She threw her arms around me again but I pulled her off. "Let's go." She hung on to my shirt as we went through the house, back outside and down the deck stairs.

"Where's Mary Ann? Did they take her? Oh my God, I don't believe this." She spotted Jamal, Emmanuel, and the blood. Her hands covered her mouth. "Oh my God. Oh, Jesus."

I pushed her down on the bottom step of the stairs. "Sit there and do not say a word. You understand me?"

She nodded and began to cry.

Mike screamed, "Where's the ambulance? Son of a bitch, how long does it take to get help out here? I can't hold this forever and I think he's going into shock."

I knelt beside Emmanuel and re-wrapped the tourniquet around his leg. "Hang in there, buddy."

"My fault, Johnny. I relaxed. I thought this was an easy gig....allowed myself to relax."

"We'll talk all about that later. Right now, we need to stop the bleeding." I turned to Brynne. "Come over here and keep this tight."

She ran over. "Sure, sure." She and Emmanuel exchanged a look and he was none too happy. Enough said.

Headlights appeared on the road. "Vehicle approaching. Not an ambulance," I said, pulling up the rifle.

Mike glanced up. "Oh, shit. Now what? Are they back?"

Emmanuel craned his neck. "My guys."

A black Chevrolet Suburban slid to a stop in front of the driveway. The doors flew open and three men jumped out. Two carried black bags. One man went to Jamal, the other went to Emmanuel and they both began medial triage.

The other man screamed, "Premises secure?"

I answered, "Yes."

A second black SUV pulled in behind the first and two more men hopped out. One went to Jamal and assisted, the other ran into the house.

A car door slammed.

Leah.

Oh, shit.

36

She had a gray blouse tucked sharply into black slacks, her hair pulled into a ponytail, was without makeup, and still looked like a million dollars; however, this was no time for niceties. Leah was all business. She barked orders to the men and then set her sights on me.

"Start talking."

"Leah, too early...compromised...not sure what happened—"

"Is that Mike's Jeep up the road?"

"We made it that far and they opened fire on us."

"You all right?"

"Physically. These two need help. Emanuel said he called an ambulance."

"Who do you think those guys are?" She pointed to her men.

Two small lanterns were now on the driveway to illuminate the makeshift emergency room. Mike held an IV bag above Jamal while the first tech administered a line. The second tech, a blond-haired guy named Tilghman, who I had met on another job, cut off Emmanuel's pant leg and secured a dressing around the wound, and now tended to the gash in his head.

"All my guys are trained in battlefield triage. You call anyone?"

"No. We should. Two dead here."

"Who are they?" she asked.

"Best guess, Bratva, or Russian ops."

"Russians? You mean from the white van?"

I recounted the backstory on how Keira, the Russians in the white van, George Ainsley, and Mary Ann Bellamy are all connected, how I figured Ainsley was the real target, and how I cooked up his disappearance to draw a reaction from Keira.

"She definitely reacted. Jesus, Johnny. You had Ainsley here, too. Why would you not tell me? We could have stashed them somewhere else or easily put additional men out here." She walked over to Jamal, and then went to Emmanuel and grilled him for a minute. She came back to me, shaking her head. "Tell me, how was this compromised?"

I threw up my hands. Leah jerked her head toward Brynne, who had retreated back to the bottom step of the stairs.

"Brynne. Mrs. Bellamy's friend. She did not want to be out here alone."

"Anyone else you forgot to tell me about?"

I shook it off. I deserved it, too.

Leah faced off to her. "Tell me what happened."

Brynne looked up at her.

"Who are you?"

Leah turned back to me with her hands parked on her hips.

"She's here to help. Tell her what you saw, if anything."

Brynne explained her version of the events, complete with tears and trembling hands.

Leah grabbed my arm and walked me to the end of the driveway. "The skinny bitch is lying. Which one was she screwing?"

"I don't know if she—"

"Which one? We don't have time and I will find out."

"I found her in Jamal's room." I explained how we observed an argument between Keira and Bellamy earlier in the evening at the Econo Lodge, tracking the van to the safe house, and how Mike and I drove into a shower of bullets.

She shook her head in dismay. "How was this compromised?"

"All I can figure is someone made a call. There is no other way she could discover Mary Ann out here. I need to see their phones."

Mike came to us, his hands covered in blood. "Leah. Sorry, tough scene."

"Thank you for what you did. You saved his life."

"He's lucky. Another inch lower, different story. The other guy?"

"Hell of a slice in his thigh and a lump on his head but he'll survive," I said.

"Mike, we'll handle your car. I doubt we want locals asking questions," she said.

He nodded. "Yeah, yeah, thanks. I'm going inside to wash up."

I shooed Brynne up to her room and told her to pack her clothes and Mary Ann's things, and bring it all down to the driveway.

Tilghman had cleaned and sutured the wound on Emmanuel's leg, patched his head, and helped me walk him up the stairs and to the sofa in the great room. Leah pulled a chair close to him. "E, you're my go-to. Right?"

"Yes, ma'am."

"You know I am grateful your injury is not worse."

"I do."

"A beach on one side, and one road in on the other. Did they come by helicopter, or did they swim up on the back of dolphins?"

The pain in his leg had to be excruciating but the sarcasm unbearable. The Army Ranger held her gaze and never wavered. "No, ma'am. I was on the front deck and heard a scream from inside. I turned and took a hit in the leg. Not sure where the shot came from. I went down. Next thing I know, I am waking up." He rubbed the lump on his head. "How I got this, I guess. Jamal must have confronted the man on the steps then went outside and dropped the one on the driveway before he went down. I found him under the front deck."

"Which places Jamal in the house when this all happened," Leah said.

Emmanuel nodded and I thought it best we move on. "The phones?"

"In my room. A strongbox in the closet."

Leah dispatched Tilghman to retrieve the box, but she was not done with Emmanuel either. "If Jamal had the woman in his room, he worked his last job."

"Yes." This time he did not look her in the eye. "I will tell him."

Tilghman came back with the metal box. Emmanuel took a key from his pocket, opened it, and pulled out three smart phones. One with a pink cover, which was Brynne's, one with a white cover, Mary Ann's, and a black phone, Ainsley's. My heart dropped to my stomach.

"This is my fault. I gave Ainsley a burner to call me and it's not here. He must have used it. Son of a bitch."

"Johnny—" Leah sat back in the chair.

"I needed to communicate with him off grid. This is on me. Emmanuel, I'm sorry."

"Not your fault. We lost focus and relaxed. Inexcusable."

"Stop the sorry," Leah snapped. "You both are culpable. But we need to move forward. E, get more men here for cleanup and to pick up Mike's Jeep."

"Will do."

She grabbed me and we went down to the front of the house. The men had Jamal loaded into the first SUV and had the dead guy in the driveway wrapped in a sheet. One of the guys came up to Leah and told her neither dead man had any identification.

My phone vibrated. A text from Eric. : *"Are you ok?"*

Jesus, I forgot about him. I sent a message back: *"Yes, call in a bit."*

"Now what?" she said. "How do we help?

Two dead, two wounded, and two missing. This night was longest of my life and it was far from over. I now had to tell Quade what went down, but leave Leah and her group out of the conversation. The last thing she wanted was the FBI sniffing around her business. The question of the night, though: why would Ainsley call Keira? No other way for Keira to find this house. Mary Ann would do as she was told, Brynne was a wild card but distracted with the booze and men, so that leaves Ainsley, who was upset with Keira. *Or so I thought.*

Leah's hand was on my shoulder. "Hey?"

"Sorry. Replaying the night."

"We'll clean up, take care of Mike's car, and get the woman home. Another car is on the way."

"I owe you."

"No, you don't. No excuse for what happened and we'll do everything in our power to help you find them."

We embraced. "Thank you. The FBI is already involved in this. I'll need to fill them in. Keep you out of it?"

"Definitely."

A third SUV pulled up with two more of her guys and she went to them with instructions.

My phone buzzed again. Eric: *"Still no Katie."*

37

Tilghman drove Mike and me back to my condo and offered to wait and help. I declined and sent him to assist at the safe house. No time for the slow elevator so we hustled up the four flights of stairs, running on adrenaline at this point. Eric was literally pacing around the room, talking to himself when we entered. Three laptops were open on the kitchen table.

"PI Dude...thank God, I am out of my mind here. What happened at the beach?"

"I'll explain later. You find Katie's car?"

"At a grocery store, not too far from here. Here, your computer." He pointed to the blinking cursor on my laptop. "I did what you said and contacted her friend Mandy, but she has not talked to her. Big mistake, because annoying Mandy has called back three times."

"Do not say a word to her. What about Keira's car?"

"No signal anymore. Nothing on the van and Bellamy went to his house."

"Stay here and monitor. We're going to Katie's car."

"Should we call Quade and Ortiz?"

"Not yet. Text me if Bellamy moves." I opened the hall closet and took a 9mm Glock from my gun safe and handed it to Mike. I clicked a new ammo clip into my

Beretta and slipped another one into my pocket. "Ready?"

I pulled the Z4 from the garage, popped the trunk and activated the handheld GPS detector. After the events of tonight, it would not surprise me if Keira stuck a transponder on me. The light on the device remained green: no tracker.

The shopping center was eight blocks from my office and Katie's red Honda was the lone car in the lot except for a Nissan compact with a flat tire, and a security vehicle parked near the entrance.

The driver's door opened and the contents of Katie's purse were spilled on the seat and her cell phone was on the floor. I put everything back into the purse.

Mike opened the passenger door and came to the same assessment as I did. "No groceries in the car so they grabbed her as she pulled in." I tried her phone but it was locked with a passcode. "Keys?" He got in and we sat with the doors open.

"No," I said. "Her wallet and money is here, so no robbery." I searched around and found her keys under the front seat. "Found them. I'll drive her car back to my garage."

"What? Partner." He put his hand on my arm. "This is a crime scene, might need to call it in. I understand the ambush on the safe house and your missing client and what we went through, but this *could* be a random abduction. Happens every day in the big city."

"We both know it's not random."

"Well, then the blonde is on the attack and the operation is blown."

"Ainsley met Katie, so he's the only one who can give her up. But he does not know I am Arthur Rhodes. So if he gave up the safe house—for whatever reason—Keira makes me as the PI Delarosa, but she shouldn't connect me as Rhodes, right?"

"Unless she tailed you from the start. Think it through. What if Ainsley was the real target? Her men bungled the hit on the road, but still maintained the tail all this time, followed him to our bar, and now you are made. Shit, we're not thinking at all—this could be a trap. You got to assume she is wise to everything."

He paused, cheeks bright red, his Irish blood boiling. I prepared for the *I told you so.*

"Why hit the safe house? Why snatch Mary Ann and Ainsley? Leverage, right? What else would it be?" Mike said. "She's hip to the whole operation, brother, no doubt in my mind. She wants something. The job will be figuring out what it is."

Flashing yellow lights lit the scene. The shopping center security guard pulled beside us in a small white pickup truck. "Need some help?"

"Daughter's car wouldn't start," I said, and waved him off, but he did not appear convinced. He stopped twenty yards away.

"Son of a bitch, the guard could be on the phone with Keira's boys now. Easy to pay him off. Hell, we're sitting here wide open." He drew in a deep breath and let it out.

"If she did tail me from the beginning, it means she played me all through the Arthur Rhodes ruse. She knew the entire time."

"I told you not to get involved with the feds. Nothing good ever comes of it." The *I told you so,* and I deserved it. "As soon as Quade finds out Katie is—I can't even say it—all hell will break loose."

"Mike, please. I will fix it." I handed him my keys. "Please."

"You move this car, you're taking any evidence with you," he said.

"I understand, but the mall cop is ready to jump into action and I'm not in the mood to be jammed up by him while Katie is being passed from Russian to Russian. We're wasting time."

"Son of a bitch. We'll both end up in Janesville over this."

He drove off in my car. I sat for a minute. This is on me and I could not allow myself one second of self-pity. When the FBI showed up, I should have bowed out, and because I did not, Katie was now in the hands of a woman who would inflict pain first and ask questions later. *If she hurts one hair on Katie's head, so help me God, I will kill her and anyone in her path, even if I have to go to Moscow to do it.* Living out my days in the joint will be worth it. The beep of a horn brought me out of my revenge-filled stupor.

"Will it start?" The security guard was beside me in his truck.

"Oh." I turned the key and the engine started. "How about that."

"Drive safe," he said.

I gave him a wave and headed to my condo.

***

Eric was asleep on the sofa when we got back to my place. I told Mike to crash in my room and he was too exhausted to object, agreeing to reconvene after a few hours of sleep. I stood in the shower for a solid five minutes, hoping the hot water would wash away the iniquity of my ineptitude. *What did I miss?*

I pulled on some sweats, closed the laptops, turned off the CD player and the lights, grabbed a bottle of bourbon and a glass, and stretched out on my balcony lounge chair. The night was cool but my adrenaline, and the unbelievable chain of events of the past six hours, had me over the edge of frustration. *Why would Ainsley call Keira and give her the location?* No explanation. The other option was she had people tailing Ainsley from the time I moved him to the safe house, which meant she played me all along. *Did she know who I was from the first meeting at the club? And what was her motivation and what does she want?* I added more of the brown liquid to my glass.

The balcony door slid open and Eric came out and sat in the other chair. For once he was subdued, not in his usual hyper state. "What happened, boss?"

I gave him the quick version: the shootout, Ainsley and Mary Ann gone, two of Leah's men wounded, Mike's car shot to hell, and now Katie, most likely being held by Keira Kaine. The tall, brutal, blonde had seized control.

"Are you going to tell her parents?" he asked.

I shook my head. "Keira will call. From what I can figure, the only reason to grab Katie was to send me a message."

"PI Dude, what kind of message?"

"To tell me she holds the power."

38

"Why would you not call me? You're going to run your own investigation? This is our case—my case—and I cannot risk it blown by you playing Rambo. You should have called me the second you knew the safe house was compromised. I could have laid a net around the area...They could be anywhere...What did you want to accomplish by hiding Ainsley? Why keep me dark...I work for the FBI for shit's sake. There are resources available to me...Three people abducted, maybe held as hostages, and no idea where they are, or where she is...And how did you sink his car into the harbor, huh? You running a goon squad?" Quade marched the length of the bar with his arms flailing one minute, hands on his hips the next.

Quade, Ortiz, Mike, Eric, and I were in McNally's at seven in the morning and needless to say, it was not a cheery start to the day. The Ainsley scheme backfired on me—and derailed his operation—or so he thought.

"We thought his wife was the target. When I realized *Ainsley* was, it made sense to remove him from the picture to draw her out. Let her think he was in danger to spark a reaction."

"Congratulations. It worked. She reacted." He took off his jacket and tie and unbuttoned his collar to prevent his neck from exploding. He put his meaty paws on two of the stools, leaned over, and stared at the floor. "Your reputation precedes you, Delarosa. Play it close to the edge, keep one foot in the shadows, do things your way, write your own rules. Probably a pain in the ass cop, too. I don't know whether to strangle you or shoot you."

I jumped from my seat and knocked over my chair. "Is that what you want to talk about, Quade? How I run my investigations? Nothing wrong with my play, but it was need to know. So why don't we forget about who's to blame and figure out how she pulled this off and where we go from here?"

He straightened and faced me.

For a change, Mike became the cool head and intervened. "Quade, he's right. Move forward—no progress this way."

Quade held up his hands. "Go ahead, genius. You tell me what we do now."

"Two things. We wait for her to call and we go squeeze Bellamy."

A knock on the front door of the restaurant. It was a delivery boy from the diner on the next block with coffee and breakfast sandwiches. We needed the time-out.

Eric spread the food out on a table then went off by himself with his computer. I unwrapped a sandwich and remembered the only thing in my stomach since lunch the day before was a half a bottle of bourbon.

"Seriously, food? This isn't a party," Quade chided. "Three people are being held against their will—by someone who could be a legit FSB asset—with secrets to a space program the entire world wants, and we have no idea where she is, and you need breakfast."

"Scott." Ortiz walked him to a chair and sat him down. "What's done is done. Solution time." She handed him a coffee, which was not smart, because the last thing I needed was Quade amped up on caffeine.

I sat down at the table with Quade, and Mike also pulled up a chair. Quade folded his arms across his chest, defiant, but listening.

"George Ainsley came here to hire me after Mary Ann was forced off the road. He whined about Keira weaseling her way into the company, the affair with Bellamy, the ruined marriage, how she wanted control of BST, force George out and deny him the credit on major new technology and a huge payday. No reason to doubt him. Next thing, you two show up and tell me he called to the Department of Defense and complained. Again, why not believe him—we all think he's a victim and is being squeezed out. Plus, he did you a favor because Keira is back on your radar."

"Yep."

"A couple of days later, I discover George's car is the same as Mary Ann's and realize he was the target from the start, and Keira's goons botched the job. But, she keeps a tail on him the entire time, which led them to me. They photographed me, and somehow took pictures of me when I first met Keira at Club Cuba—"

"When you were Arthur Rhodes." Quade open a sandwich and talked through his chewing "Son of a bitch. We think she's taking the bait and meanwhile, she's three moves ahead of us."

"She compares pictures and is wise to the scheme from the jump," I said.

Ortiz slid her chair to the table. "If all that is true, she has more help than the two morons we saw at the motel. They are not smart enough to follow you to the safe house or do professional surveillance."

"We had counter-surveillance all around the club and the Greek diner and they still got pictures, which means they are real pros. Confirms what we believed from New York. She's FSB, no doubt." Quade devoured a second sandwich.

"Say all that's true," I said. "Then why did Ainsley give up the house? He hates Keira for what she is doing to the company, the Bellamys' marriage, and his payday. I don't understand."

"Unless it was his way to cripple her? He figures if he calls her and draws her out, we can wrap her up. Only he underestimated her, like we did," Mike said.

"No." Ortiz paced the room. "He tried to save himself. He calls Keira, tells her where they are so he can gain favor with her and hope to get his piece of the pie. Otherwise, no shot at the money or the glory."

"Mamacita is correct," Eric said, never taking his eyes from his laptop. "The old dude's cash is history after this fiasco. He's at the end of the line."

Quade huffed. "Hacker dude, speaks. You've been too quiet today. You're right, though. You and Mamacita."

Ortiz smirked and feigned a slap to Quade's face. "What I don't get, when she uncovered Johnny and the whole Arthur Rhodes scheme, she did not spook and run. She goes on the offensive. Why? She knew Ainsley was mad and blew it up to the DOD. She's aware Mary Ann hired a private investigator, and must figure us feds are here or why else the Arthur Rhodes ruse, and then grabs three hostages? Doesn't make sense. What's her end goal?"

Ortiz, the smartest one in the room, asked the question that hung over us—what was Keira's strategy? All the cards were in her hand and I don't even know the game.

"Whatever it is, we are still in play, Quade. It's her move," I said. "She'll call today."

"She better because I can't sit on this. A few hours at best before I notify my ASAC, and that is stretching it," he said. "Mike, Eric, do not leave this bar. Maria will be here, business as usual. Remember, she is watching."

"Eric, Bellamy's car?" I asked.

"Pulled into BST ten minutes ago."

"Ready, Quade?"

"Now you want to include me?"

"No choice. You're the only way in."

39

Quade's FBI credentials sent us through the guard shack at Bellamy Space without an issue. We parked in a small lot in the front of the building, next to Bellamy's green Range Rover. The head of security for the company, a middle-aged man named Foster—short, stubby, with a crew cut, gold wire-framed glasses, and an ill-fitting black suit—met us in the lobby.

Quade flashed his badge. "Mr. Foster, we are here about—"

"About Mr. Ainsley. I can only tell you what I told the local police the other day. Quiet guy, quirky, odd. Employees here don't tell me much but I make it a point to be friendly, and when you're friendly, people like to talk. I don't understand who would want to hurt the old man, unless, you know, with all the top-secret stuff, conspiracy theories and such, folks love to speculate. Me, personally, I don't believe it, but there are nut jobs in this world—I don't have to tell you guys—and Mr. Bellamy is a big player. Maybe someone tried to compromise Ainsley and the old guy wouldn't budge. Just an assumption, but me, I keep my mouth shut."

Foster was an investigator's wet dream. I caught Quade's eye and could tell he was chomping at the bit, but I went first. "Foster, how many years in law enforcement?"

"This is my twelfth, sir, and my second year with Bellamy and damn proud of it. Tough to catch on here, too. Requires a federal background check, which takes a solid year to complete."

"You wearing a side arm?"

He flipped open his suit jacket to reveal a holstered pistol. "Glock 9."

"Your men all carry?"

"No, only me, and the guys in uniform who work the front gate and our outside perimeter patrols. We have a separate team who monitor the security cameras and make interior rounds. They don't carry."

"You all work for the Federal Protective Service?"

"Yep, sure do. We are not normally assigned to contractors, but this building and the operation is classified."

Quade couldn't wait any longer. "Well, Foster, I am damn glad we got a guy like you on our side. We need some information and I'm sure you can help."

"Of course." Foster beamed. "Let's move someplace where we can talk." He ushered us down a corridor to a small conference room and we sat around an oval table. "Coffee, water?"

"No, no, we'll only take a minute," Quade said.

"Anything I can do to help a brother in blue—"

"Mr. Foster, we're here to see Mr. Bellamy, but before we do that, what can you tell us about Keira Kaine?"

"Ms. Kaine, huh? Nice lady, always speaks to me. She and I started about the same time. Senior executive. Some say she is the mastermind behind the new project. Some type of breakthrough for the company."

"Other employees talk about her?"

Foster smiled. "Well, she's an attractive woman, looks like a fashion model, so of course all the women gossip. What can I say? A little skinny for my taste."

"They gossip about her and Bellamy?"

"I don't pay close attention to rumors. Prefer dealing with facts."

"George Ainsley is missing and Bellamy is a contractor for the Department of Defense. Those are facts. I want full disclosure and nothing leaves this room," Quade said. "Understood?"

Foster nodded, took a moment. "Well, the word is Bellamy's wife left him because of her."

"Ever see anything that would make you suspect them of having an affair?"

"No, never."

"Hard to believe. You watch the security monitors all day, right?"

"Yep."

"Nothing? They ever stay late, that sort of thing?"

"Never."

"Is she here today?"

"No, haven't seen her in a few days."

Quade let a minute go by. "Mr. Foster, I respect the fact you are loyal to Bellamy. No doubt in my mind he's been good to you, but you are chief of security for a government contractor with a top-secret clearance. Any inappropriate behavior at the executive level could trigger a forfeiture of the company's contract and the next thing you know, you're a night watchman at Walmart." Foster shifted in his chair. "Remember where your paycheck comes from. I guarantee Bellamy won't protect you so I suggest you be on the right side of this."

He thought for a second, cleared his throat. "Between us guys?"

"Of course," I said.

"Never fails to amaze me the stupid things people do in the name of love—or lust. Cameras in every corner of this building." He pointed to the ceiling and the smoked-glass sphere above us. "One day, we observe the two of them walking along a corridor, and all of a sudden, he grabs her hand and pulls her into a conference room. We switch to the room, he yanks up her skirt and right there on camera, he bangs her on the table. All on video. Then they straightened their clothes and went about their business. We had six guys crowded around the screens and must have watched it twenty times." He chuckled. "We were proud of him, too. He hit it hard and we always thought he was a bit of a milquetoast. Inappropriate behavior, hell yeah."

"Thank you. You did the right thing by telling us. Confirms their relationship, if nothing else," Quade said.

"One more thing. I lied. She's a world-class bitch. The entire company hates her. She treated everyone terrible, especially George. Supposedly, he constantly challenged her but Bellamy stood by her. As soon as word broke he was missing, the first thing we all thought—Keira Kaine."

"That she had something to do with his disappearance?"

He shrugged. "People are capable of anything these days."

"Good intel. We'll talk again." Quade handed him a business card. "You hear anything, do not hesitate." Foster slipped the card into his shirt pocket. "Now, we'd like to talk to Bellamy."

"He's not here."

"What? His car is out front."

"Oh, yeah. Sometimes he asks us to go to his place and bring his car over. Every so often he'll come in with Ms. Kaine—sorry, should have mentioned that earlier—and won't have a car to go home. So we go to his house and drive his car back here—"

"And you moved his car this morning?"

"Yep. One of my guys."

"Who drove it? I want to talk to him."

Foster made a call and a minute later, a tall, skinny kid of around twenty-five came into the conference room. Foster introduced him as Nick. He wore black pants cinched tight around his waist with a black belt, and a white, short-sleeve shirt at least two sizes too big, with a BST Security patch on the left sleeve.

"Nick, these two are FBI and have some questions," Foster said. Nick sat at the table and clasped his hands together, his fingers locked so tight his knuckles were white.

Quade opened a notepad. "When you went to Mr. Bellamy's house today to get his car, did you notice anything out of the ordinary?"

"No. No, sir."

"What exactly do you do when you go for his car?"

"Mr. Foster here gives me the keys, one of the guys drives me over, and I drive Mr. Bellamy's car back."

"His car in his garage?" I asked.

"Yes."

"So you know the alarm code?"

"Yes."

Foster jumped in. "No way, boys. I can't do it. You need a warrant for that. Thanks, Nick."

Nick took his cue and wasted no time leaving the room.

"Understood, Foster. Where is Bellamy then?"

"No idea. He does not tell us on a day-by-day. He's usually here, or at a meeting off campus, whatever. He could be at the warehouse."

"Warehouse?"

"Yeah, a few miles from here," he said.

"What happens at the warehouse?"

"Storage. They build satellite prototypes here but the materials are stored there."

Quade flipped open a notebook. "Address?"

"Umm, the exact address is in my office, but it's two miles on the same road."

"We'll stop by there."

Foster beamed. "Not without me."

40

Quade and I followed Foster the two miles to the BST warehouse. It was a single story, white cinder block building, with two loading docks on the right side as we approached. No cars in the parking lot or any trucks in sight. We parked beside the front gate.

The guard came out to greet us, a younger guy of thirty or so. "Hey, Mr. Foster."

"Sanderson, these gentlemen are with the FBI. Have you seen Mr. Bellamy today?"

"No, not at all. Been quiet."

Quade flipped open his badge. "Special Agent Quade. You keep a record of everyone who goes through?"

"Of course." He stood with his hands on his hips.

"Sanderson, the log." Foster rolled his eyes.

"Sure, sure." He was back a moment later with a log book. "Like I said, quiet. Nobody today."

Foster took the book and traced his finger down the page. "Only person in the last twenty-four hours is Miss Kaine at eight thirty last night." He looked at Sanderson. "Were you working when she came through?"

"No, my shift ended at three. Mackey was on after me."

"Does Ms. Kaine often come to this building?" Quade asked.

"Umm, not too much. I've only seen her a few times during the day."

"Foster, does she have access?"

"Sure, vice president of the company. She comes over now and then—inventory, I think. I don't keep track of what she does when she is here, only know they keep the solar panels and other materials they use to build the prototypes."

"Security inside?"

"Only one man who monitors video then makes hourly rounds, plus a man out here at the gate. All I need. Not much happens unless we get a delivery."

"So when she comes over, is she escorted while in the building?"

"No, no reason. All raw materials, lightweight metals. You know I can't say much."

"So you'll have video of her inside the warehouse?" I said.

"Of course." Foster got to where I was going and held up a hand. "Pushing it. Need to come up with a warrant. Besides, I thought this was about Ainsley?"

"Running down every angle, that's all," Quade said. "Any chance you can watch the video and tell us if you see something unusual?"

"I suppose. Not sure what I'm looking for."

"Anything you think is out of the ordinary."

"I can only review video back in my office, so I'll call you if anything jumps out."

My best ally is my gut instinct and it has yet to fail me. "What about the man who was on duty last night? Can we talk to him?"

Sanderson spoke up. "Mackey. He works three to eleven, but...umm...he called me at home. Said he had an emergency and asked if I could cover for him until Stanley got here at eleven. I wasn't doing nothing so I came in."

"That all needs to go through me." Foster said. "You guys can't switch shifts without my permission."

"Sorry. It was last minute."

I pointed to the cameras mounted around the front gate. "What about video?"

Foster sucked in a deep breath and motioned to Sanderson. "Pull it up."

We crammed into the guard booth and watched the video of Keira, in her Mercedes, coming through the checkpoint at eight thirty. We spotted her and Bellamy after ten at the motel, and the safe house was hit at eleven. "What time did Mackey call you?"

"Around nine. I got here at nine thirty," Sanderson said.

Foster and Sanderson both wore their BST company ID badge around their neck with their name and photo on it. "Foster, you keep employee ID pictures on file?"

"Yeah, sure do. Need to access it from my office computer."

"Send his picture to Quade as soon as you can."

"You think Mackey is involved—"

"Again, all leads." Quade cut him off. "You've been very helpful, but we need a favor. Can you call Bellamy? His number in your phone?"

"Sure."

"What is it?"

"I'm not comfortable giving out Mr. Bellamy's cell phone—"

"Foster." Quade snapped. "How long do you think it will take for my office to get Bellamy's phone number? Huh?"

"I'm sure you guys—"

"Right. So you are either working with me, or against me." Quade towered over Foster by a solid six inches. "What's it going to be?"

Foster pulled up the number on his phone and Quade jotted it on his note pad, along with Foster's. He stepped out of the booth and placed a call.

A moment later, he was back. "Okay, Foster. In one minute I want you to call Bellamy and if he answers, keep him on the line as long as possible."

Sanderson's eyes went wide. "What's going on?"

Foster glared at him and he shrunk back into a corner. He nodded to Quade. "I'm going to step out because I'll be too nervous."

"Do not say we are here. Tell him his car was brought over but you noticed an oil leak and keep him talking." Quade made another call. "Ortiz, are they ready?" He signaled Foster to dial.

The one thing we learned about Foster was that he could talk. Bellamy answered and Foster rambled on about the car and what they should do. After two minutes, Quade gave us a thumbs-up and Foster ended the call.

"Good work."

"He sounded drunk," Foster said.

"Makes sense. They pegged him to a bar downtown." Quade turned to me. "Ready?"

We both shook Foster's hand and told him he did great and to send us the video of Keira in the warehouse and a picture of Mackey. His moment of glory with the FBI must have empowered him because when we pulled off, he was screaming at Sanderson.

41

Ortiz relayed directions to Bellamy's location as we drove. Foster came through and sent video of Keira photographing the inventory in the warehouse. He also sent an employee ID photo of Victor Mackey, and because my gut never betrays me, I was not surprised to see he was the same man who caused the distraction by smoking in Club Cuba during my first Keira meeting. He was also the dead man I stepped over in the driveway of the safe house. *Who else in Bellamy Space worked for the Russians?*

More information came from Ortiz. Mackey's real name was Alekzander Kazakova, a confirmed member of Bratva, with addresses in New York City and Paterson, New Jersey. She ran his local address and it turned out to be a vacant lot near the docks. She and Eric were now checking all background sources on Mackey. He made number four in Russian operatives, including Keira and her two flunkies, Vlasova and Makarov, on this case. If Quade's investigation and presumption is correct, she established herself in the United States, and being the dutiful FSB operative, loyal to the twenty-first century motherland, worked her way into the target company, impressed her handlers, and they awarded her with support in the form of Mackey and the two goons. The looming question: was her end game now in play, and if so, what was it?

The coordinates led us to the Dark Side bar, the place where Katie and I first photographed Keira and Bellamy with my camera pen. This time, he was parked on a stool. The same bartender was on duty and he gave me a second glance when we came in, as if he recognized me.

Quade flashed his badge in front of Bellamy's face. "Thomas Bellamy? FBI. Need to ask you a few questions."

Bellamy turned around and faced us. "Well, well, the feds." He slurred his words, already half in the bag. Quade took him by the arm and led him to a table in the back.

"When did he get here?" I said to the bartender.

"Hour or so. He was waiting in the parking lot when I opened. Hey, weren't you in here before?"

"He do any talking?"

"Nah, mumbled stuff about his business and how he got screwed...I barely listened. I have guys in here every day complaining about their lives."

"He comes in with a blonde woman. She been here lately?"

"You *were* in here. I remember. Had a blonde of your own."

"Answer my question."

"No. Not on my shift, anyhow."

"How many drinks has he had?"

He shrugged. "Two, three...I'm not sure."

"Bring some coffee." I joined Quade and Bellamy at the table.

"Mr. Bellamy says he has not seen Keira for three days." Quade had a notepad open in front of him.

"Really?" I said. "Swear I saw you two at an Econo Lodge outside of town last night."

Bellamy cleared his throat and straightened in his chair in an effort to shake off the booze. "You want to tell me what this is about?"

"Your business."

"What about it?"

"Let's start with George Ainsley. Presumed dead. Any ideas?"

"I told the police everything I know. Which is nothing."

"Then the matter with your wife. She left you because of your affair with Ms. Kaine."

"Marriage was over long before Keira joined the company."

"Mary Ann doesn't see it that way."

"So, I had an affair. Happens. When did the FBI start doing divorce work?"

Quade leaned halfway across the table. "You're a government contractor with a top-secret clearance and new technology that other countries would love to take a peek at, your lead scientist is probably at the bottom of the harbor, you're sleeping with your senior VP, and your wife wants a divorce." Quade reached across and jabbed a finger in his chest. "That's when the FBI shows up."

Bellamy got the point. His head down, he sunk back in the chair. "Now what?"

The bartender served up three cups of coffee.

"Tell us about Keira Kaine," Quade said.

He went through the same story Ainsley and Mary Ann told. How they met at a conference, how she impressed him, and how he invited her to join BST. "Everything was fine at first. A brilliant woman; worked well with George. Then she and I began to work together and we clicked. We spoke the same language about everything. The late nights led to later nights, and eventually we fell in love. At least I did. She told me she did, too. Now, I'm not so sure."

"How did Ainsley react to your relationship?" I asked.

"Furious with me. Felt I jeopardized everything he and I built. I figured he was envious of Keira and felt he got shoved aside. All untrue."

"You aware he complained to the DOD?"

"What? No. Why would he do that?"

"He thought you showed weakness and poor judgment with your involvement with her, and feared you jeopardized the future of the company."

"Ridiculous."

"Ever observe her doing anything out of the ordinary? Work late? Meet with anyone you did not know?"

"Never. Why?"

Quade closed his note book and laid his pen on the table. "Mr. Bellamy, we have reason to believe Ms. Kaine could be passing classified information about your technology to another country."

"Preposterous."

"You sure? Our intelligence tells us otherwise."

Bellamy loosened his tie and unbuttoned his collar, ran his hand through his hair. "There was one time...I overheard her on the phone, and she spoke in a different language. It sounded like Russian, but I don't speak it so I'm guessing."

"Did you say anything?"

"No, but it gave me pause, made me wonder if George was correct in all his suspicions."

"He said he was suspicious?"

"Not that she passed secrets. He was upset she had so much control. I thought he was jealous of her position. I always credited him with the advancements we made, but I wanted a young, dynamic personality as the face of the company and she was perfect."

"When did you overhear her conversation? The one in Russian?"

"Few weeks ago, I think. Same time everything blew up with Mary Ann. When she got in the car accident and then moved out."

My turn. "You heard her speaking Russian and never questioned her?"

He shook his head.

"We observed you several times over the past two weeks with Keira at motels. We have photographic evidence of the two of you together, which I'm sure Mary Ann's divorce lawyer will love, but it always seemed like an argument. Want to explain?"

His eyes went wide. "Mary Ann had me followed?" He sipped at his coffee. "Wow, she actually did something. I didn't think she had the balls."

"Well, Bellamy, you arrogant prick, you can only humiliate a woman so much."

"Hey!"

He came out of his chair as if he was coming across the table at me, but Quade's giant body came up first. "Sit back down. You don't move unless I give you permission. Got it?"

He sat, but still had a hint of defiance in his voice. "If all this was true, her colluding with another government, why didn't she leave with the technology? She had ample time and resources."

"How do we know she didn't?" I said.

He did not respond. I wondered whether he was calculating his next move, or realizing what an idiot he was and accepting defeat.

After a minute: "I trusted her. Everything was perfect. I experienced things on a professional and personal level that I thought would never happen. The company was...we were going to be superstars in the world of space technology. Life-changing technology, not just for us, but for the nation. And being with her...intimately, was more than amazing."

His chin dropped to his chest, but we could not allow him to sink too far. We might need him to help us.

"We don't know the damage, if any," Quade said. "You'll go back to your house and a couple of agents will remain with you until we reach some conclusion on this mess."

"I need to go to my office—"

"What you need and what's going to happen are two different things. Don't move." Quade got up from the table and made a phone call.

"Have you tried calling her this morning?" I asked.

"Yes. She won't answer."

Quade and I decided on the way over to not tell him his wife was also missing. We did not want him to react, or decide to become a hero in his mind and tip off Keira, which could put Mary Ann and Katie in more danger.

Quade requested several more agents to assist and we sat with Bellamy until Ortiz arrived. She loaded him into her car with instructions to stay with him at his house until the other agents show up.

We were back in Quade's car when the burner phone vibrated in my pocket.

"Well, talk about timing," I said, showing Quade the number on the phone.

I answered, "Hello."

"Mr. Rhodes, time for us to meet."

42

The team was in high gear, all throwing out options and opinions on how to proceed with my meeting, now scheduled for ten that evening in a small city park near Santorini's, the Greek breakfast place. The call with Keira was brief. I was to wait on a bench next to the playground.

Quade and I had brought Ortiz and Eric up to speed on our Bellamy interrogation. The two agents proceeded to clash on how to handle my safety, surveillance of the park, how many men they needed, and how many they could grab on short notice. I suggested it might be necessary to involve the PCPD, but Quade refused. He spouted national security mumbo jumbo and how the local police do not hold clearances.

We were crashed around my kitchen table—Eric, the FBI, and me. Quade wanted me to wear a wire, which I quickly shot down as a death wish.

"We can embed it in your jacket collar. They'll never find it."

"No. Too risky. They can scan me and pick up transmission signals. Same with the GPS button."

"You need some electronics on you."

"My phone."

"Right," Eric said. "They'll expect him to have a phone, so I'll follow him until the bad dudes take his celly away."

Quade checked to Ortiz and she nodded an approval. "No devices, phone only."

Ortiz continued, "I don't want you to drive there. We should drop you a few blocks away and you walk. That way you can sense the vibe on the street, check counter-surveillance, see if you catch a tail. We have men on the block now, scouting, securing a vantage point."

"What if it's a decoy? She could be sending me there as a diversion."

"We thought about that, too," Quade said. "Not much we can do. No ransom instructions, no communication to Bellamy, no activity at her apartment. NSA reports no extra chatter. All too quiet, and that bothers me."

"Maybe she makes her ransom demand through me tonight?"

Ortiz shook her head. "It doesn't make sense, after the attack on the house, she would risk bringing us to her?"

"Mama's right." Eric bounced around the room. "None of this makes sense." We all turned our attention to our boy genius and awaited the wisdom that was about to pour forth. "Let's think this through...she had access to the technology, but...what? Nothing. Bellamy had a point—she had the resources to leave with the loot months ago, but stayed. Why? You dudes observe her and Tommy boy arguing more than once, why? Super-agent Quade tells us she is a Russian sleeper agent—so freakin' cool—but anyhow, old man Ainsley clues her in about PI Dude and the feds hot on her ass, then he rats out the safe house so she can attack and now holds hostages—"

Quade had no patience. "We don't need a history of the case—"

"Let him finish, he's building to a point. I hope," Ortiz said.

"Thank you, Mama. Me and you—two bodies, one soul."

"No, we are not. Get to the point."

"It appears she's in control, the hostages and all, but she's on defense. Using hostages as protection. So, WWJBD."

We all said, "Huh?" at the same time.

"WWJBD. What Would James Bond Do? When Bond gets squeezed, he goes on offense, right? Not defense. My point is this: I say she's stuck. She's cornered, so we move in while we can."

We stared at him and allowed his peculiar 007 reference to sink in. However, he was dead on. She *was* stuck.

"He's right. Go back to what Bellamy said. Why not leave when she had the chance?" I said.

Eric wasn't finished. "Something else—you said she was photographing the inventory? She knows damn well that you guys will eventually see the video. It was all for show." He stretched his skinny body out on my sofa. "Thank you, and PI Dude, I think I earned a permanent job with the firm."

Quade pulled a beer out of the fridge. "No way. You wasted our time, hacker dude."

Ortiz helped herself to her own beer. "No, he didn't. He's close. Something happened, and we don't know what. You saw arguments with Bellamy, so she's mad at him for some reason, and at the same time Ainsley blows it all up by complaining to Washington, which brings us in, and her scheme is shot to hell."

My turn to be animated and spout a theory. "Yes, right. She's exposed, doesn't have the technology, and needs leverage to get herself out of the quicksand, which is closing in and pulling her down fast."

"PI Dude, nice metaphor. Any food in here?"

"Yeah, I'm starving, too. We did not eat all day," Quade said. "Okay, he makes a good point—she's jammed. What I still don't understand—where are her handlers? Why not exfiltrate her when it all got hot?"

"No technology, no worth. She has no value without the space plans, so the boys in Moscow turned their back," I said.

"Damn, Johnny." Quade marched around the condo. "If you're correct, and she is now dead to the motherland, and if they abandoned her, her only recourse is to—"

"Flip." Ortiz slammed her hand on the table. "Jesus, that's it. She's going to use the hostages to negotiate a deal for herself."

"Again, you are welcome," Eric yelled from the sofa.

"Seems rather dramatic, holding hostages—if they are hostages, we have no idea at this point—why not walk into the FBI and turn herself in?"

"She needs something, dudes."

"Eric is correct. Why would someone in her spot hold a hostage? To gain, what? Money? If her cover is blown, which it is, and Russia turned their back, she needs protection."

We needed a break and all sat silent. Eric called down to the bar for sandwiches to be sent up, and none of us moved until Mike came in twenty minutes later. We went through various scenarios with him and he offered his opinion, which matched our consensus. She must be backed into a corner and the only way out was to hold some leverage.

I rejected Ortiz's suggestion they drive me within a few blocks of the park then walk. If she made me as Delarosa, then we assumed I would be tailed as soon as I left this building. The smartest play would be for me to go alone and sit and wait as instructed.

After we demolished the sandwiches, we decided figuring out Keira's motive was a waste of our time and we turned to the strategy for tonight's rendezvous between her and Arthur Rhodes.

Ortiz and Quade agreed to station themselves three blocks from the park. I would leave my phone on and Eric would monitor from my condo and maintain an open line between him and the agents. We ordered him to stay put and to not leave the condo under any circumstances. Quade also agreed to keep counter-surveillance to minimum. If she truly was FSB and had support, a man would be tucked in every doorway, hidden in every shadow, and watching from every rooftop. Experts in surveillance tradecraft, they would sniff out a FBI agent in seconds.

At dusk, I wandered to my balcony with a double pour of bourbon in a glass. Over the course of my career, I ran undercover ops many times. Posed as a drug dealer, junkie, gun runner, pimp, john, bookie, and even as a fence trying to unload a boxcar full of televisions. Every time my heart pounded, my nerves charged, and most times the sting went down as designed. This one, though, I'm not so sure. People I set out to protect are now held unprotected. *How did I fail them?*

Ainsley was an enigma and I was not sure what to think about him. *Why would he tip off Keira to the safe house? Was he working for her or against her?* I'm dying for that answer.

Katie consumed my mind since last night. *Where was she at this moment? Was she hurt, under duress, in pain? Was she locked in some room, or tied to chair like the first time I met her? Was she hungry, thirsty, cold, naked, or clothed?* Before I met Katie I never dreamed of someone working with me on a case. Now I can't think of working a case without her.

Mary Ann Bellamy. The ultimate innocent victim. All she did was take action against her sorry excuse of a husband; now she finds herself at the mercy of a woman who would inflict pain on a whim and take pleasure in doing so.

Eric was inside, still stretched out on the sofa, catching a nap before tonight's fun. I smiled at the thought of his wacky, but uniquely likable personality and brilliant mind.

WWJBD? He would not be melancholy and wallow in self-pity. He would be tying the perfect bowtie, slipping on his expensive, expertly tailored black tuxedo jacket, tucking the Walther PPK in his shoulder holster, and then stopping by the hotel bar for a martini, shaken not stirred.

I toasted 007 and drank my bourbon.

Katie and Mary Ann, I'm on my way.

43

A damp, misty fog rolled in from the ocean, God's way of adding atmosphere to the clandestine meeting with Keira, and added a wet shine to the streets. I took a cab from McNally's to six blocks from Greek Town Park and walked the rest of the way. Every man, woman, or child on the street seemed suspicious. My nerves pinged on high alert, but I decided to see this through and could not turn back. I had no choice: my client, and a person I held dear to me, faced danger and it was my job to bring this to a safe completion.

I wondered how long Keira would play out my Arthur Rhodes persona. Would she keep the ruse going, or upend my deception and challenge me, or would she come clean and use me as her ticket out of her botched mission to steal technology from the United States and beg for a deal? Or, would they flat out kill me and leave me at the mercy of our Lord? Then I'd need all the help I could get.

Eric and Ortiz pulled up city maps of the park before I left to aid in reconnaissance. Two acres of a grassy recreation area with a children's playground and soccer field at one end, and a small wooded patch with walking paths at the other. I sat on the bench near the playground as instructed.

Forty yards from me, a homeless person, or a bum in my day, was bundled up and stretched out on a bench. No other souls in sight. Eric manned our communications center back in the condo and Quade and Ortiz waited in a car some blocks away. Ten o'clock came and went. I had my phone in my hand and my Beretta in the waistband of my jeans. At ten twenty, the homeless man threw off a blanket and stood, glanced around, and shuffled in my direction, the first time I ever prayed for a person to actually be homeless and coming to ask for handout. I moved my gun into my jacket pocket.

At fifteen yards, he said, "Hey, buddy, can you help me out?"

"Not tonight."

He was now within twenty feet and his gait changed from a shuffle to upright, swift, and I was his target. I stood and pulled the gun just as an arm came from behind me and knocked it from my hand. I turned and swung but the homeless guy was now on me and we both went to the ground. I landed on my stomach, with him on my back.

All his weight pressed on my back, pinning me down. He said, "Do it," to the other man and then a sharp sting to my neck. *Did they get me with a needle?* I mustered some strength and bucked up and kicked out, scrambled to my feet. *Or did he let me up?* It was too dark to find my gun. *Or did they have it?* I squared off to both of them, but they stood there, watching me. A stiffness in my neck traveled down my body...they got me with something. A dizziness swirled in my head. *Where's my gun?* The bench a few feet from me and I wanted to sit. *What? Who?* I stepped forward but my legs did not work and I fell to the grass.

I could see and hear but my body would not move. They turned me onto my back. "Find his phone." Light mist sparkled in the glow of a streetlamp. They tugged at my shoes...stripped me of my clothes. I tried to shake off the paralysis, but nothing...naked on the wet grass...cold. More tugging and pulling and now no longer wet. *Did they put new clothes on me? Quade, where are you? Are you seeing this?* A flash of clarity and I figure they will leave my clothes and phone on the bench, as if I never left that spot. *Eric will never know...*

I floated in the air. *Being carried?* Treetops...the night sky...crystal raindrops in the shine of arc lights. We stopped...doors opened and closed. I was on my back...the cargo area of a van. *The white van?* My arms and legs frozen. The men sat in the front and did not speak. We were moving—to where? Bumps, stops, turns...*keep track,* I told myself...*need to tell Quade.* A cell phone rang. One man said two words I did not understand. *On my way to somewhere to never be found...Katie, hold on, I'm coming.* I tried to lift my head...*so dizzy...*then a thick fog of black rolled over me.

***

My head throbbed, my arms and wrists hurt, but I welcomed the pain because feeling was back in my body. I opened my eyes to the harsh glare of a light bulb hanging from a ceiling. I blinked them into focus and scanned around. *A basement of a house?* I stood upright, my feet on the floor but secured. My arms and legs outstretched, in a standing, spread-eagle position. Thin ropes wrapped around each wrist, pulling my arms up and out, tied to eye screws in the rafters above. A rope was around my right ankle with the other end fastened to a steel support pole. My left leg was tethered to an old workbench.

And I was naked.

Talk about being in a vulnerable position. I yanked on the ropes but it only made the knots tighter. Thoughts raced through my head: *last night, drugged, brought here in the van, now hung up like a lamb for slaughter.*

Dirty, dingy, damp, and musty. Filthy concrete floor, boxes stacked in one corner, and two old bicycles under a set of wooden stairs to my left. To my right, a furnace and water heater. A small window sat high on the far wall. Still dark outside. *How long was I strung up here?* Nothing good went through my brain. *Were Katie and Mary Ann also held in this house? How long did Quade and Ortiz sit and wonder why I never moved from the bench? How long did Eric stare at the blinking cursor indicating my phone still in the park? Did they think Keira met me and we sat there for our meeting? Did the FBI have any visual surveillance on me?* My abduction probably took less than one minute. At what point did they decide enough was enough and move in? By that time, I was on my back in a van and on my way to...where?

The muscles in my arms ached.

Ignore it, Delarosa. Pain is the least of your problems at the moment. Listen, remember everything.

Nothing, no sounds, only the occasional creak of an old house. I listened for voices, a television, snoring—anything to tell me someone else was here.

What if I am alone? What if they tied me up here and are not coming back? Three days without water, I'm dead.

I had to calm myself and think. I took in some deep breaths, scanned around the basement, hoping to spot something...anything.

A movement on the floor across from me. A mouse.

Are you serious, God?

I watched him duck between several cartons. A minute later, he came back out, sniffed the air, scurried toward the furnace. *Did he pick up my scent yet?* The hair stood on the back of my neck.

C'mon, Delarosa, a mouse?

I decided to slowly remember any and everything in the room. An old bow saw, the kind for cutting small tree branches, hung on a pegboard on the wall behind the workbench. The taut ropes held my legs apart; the only option was to pull on the ropes around my wrists. The house was old and I might be able to work the eye screw loose. I began with my right hand and it hurt like hell, but I got up a rhythm and yanked and pulled, the rope cutting deeper into my wrist with each effort. My heart pounded; my chest heaved; sweat rolled down my back, my face, off my forehead and into my eyes. I blinked it out and looked back up to the eye bolt. Nothing.

I switched to my left arm and jerked on the rope as hard as I could, straining, clenched teeth grinding through the pain in my wrist, determined not to quit until the goddam bolt pulled from the wood.

I stopped.

Footsteps on the floor above me. *Did I miss someone come in because of the noise I was making?*

Then, a voice.

Keira.

44

The footsteps traveled back and forth across the wooden floor above me while she spoke, in Russian, or some Eastern European language. It was not English, and in my current predicament, it didn't matter whether it was Martian. I only heard her voice so I figured it was a phone call, and from what I could determine, she was not happy. Regardless the language, a man could always tell when a woman was upset.

The call ended, and then silence. No movement. *What was she doing? Sending a text?* After what seemed like an eternity passed, the footfalls resumed, moving to my left. A door creaked and a light clicked on in the stairwell. Black boots came down the steps.

She dressed for the part, black everything. Boots, jeans, and T-shirt. She stopped a few feet in front of me, crossed her arms over her chest and smiled. "Mr. Rhodes. You are certainly in a bit of a situation."

"You want to cut me down and explain what this is about?"

"You lied to me. Imagine my surprise when I find out your name is Delarosa and you're a private investigator."

"No idea what you are talking about. Cut these ropes."

"An amateur try at best. You were convincing, but way out of your league. You stepped out of your safe, cozy world of background checks and cheating husbands, and decided to swim in the deep end and look what happened. You're hooked like a mackerel ready to be gutted." She came closer and put her hand on my chest. "Handsome man, though." She traced her hand from my chest to my stomach, took a step back and studied everything below my navel. "Not bad, for an American."

"What do you want, Nadia?" No sense in keeping up the Rhodes fiasco.

"Nadia? Well, your friends did some digging."

"They're on their way."

"Johnny—can I call you Johnny?—that's cute. We both know they're not coming. They'll never find you—hell, even I got lost finding this place. The rats will get to your carcass before the FBI does."

"What do you want?"

She walked to the workbench and picked up a screwdriver and pointed it at me. "It is not what I want, it's what I need. Can you help me with what I need? Huh, Johnny?"

"Sure. Cut me down and we'll work it out. Whatever you need."

"A desperate plea from a man a precarious position."

"Let me help you. I'll tell the FBI you want a deal."

"A deal? You talk like I committed a crime."

"Where's Mary Ann Bellamy, and Ainsley? And my assistant, Katie?"

"Are you serious? First, I don't know any Katie. Second, I would not waste my time on the little twit Mary Ann. And poor Mr. Ainsley, the crazy old coot. Time for the old folk's home before he embarrasses himself."

"Are you holding them in this house?"

She smiled, pulled the bow saw off the wall and held it up. "I could untie you, but what I planned is so much more fun."

"Not too late. Let's talk about the options before you're in too deep."

"Options?" She rummaged around on the workbench and came back to me with the saw in one hand and a pair of pliers in the other. "The options are whether to crush your balls or cut them off. Any preference?"

The muscles in my arms ached. Sweat dripped off my face, and rolled down my back. "Decision I prefer to avoid. What do you want from me?"

She tossed the saw into a corner, then wiped the sweat off my brow with one finger, stuck it in her mouth and sucked, and then wrapped her arms around my neck and whispered into my ear. "Tell me that wasn't sexy." She slapped my butt with the pliers. "The problem is, they say I have a sadistic streak." She stepped back to face me again. "Maybe I do, but I think of it as a way to create respect. Keep your enemies off-balance, right?"

She opened the pliers and put them around Little Johnny and gave a slight squeeze. A shiver ran up my spine. "Oh, that would hurt, huh?"

"You don't want to do this."

"You're not having fun?" She removed the pliers, but cupped my balls in her hand and squeezed. "I like a man who has balls. You weren't afraid to take a chance." I gasped, my chest heaved, my heart pounded. "But you deceived me, and I do not appreciate being played."

Think, man. Think.

She squeezed harder.

Oh God...please...

"Ainsley," I said. "It was all about Ainsley. The FBI wanted to separate you from Bellamy and offer you a deal. I can explain."

She let go. "Funny what motivates a person. Go ahead, explain."

"Mary Ann hired me to get proof of your affair. Then Ainsley showed up in my office wanting me to investigate you. He had complained to Washington about you and Bellamy and the DOD was concerned he was a loose cannon with important technology on the line. So the feds wanted you and the technology, but didn't want Bellamy and Ainsley. So they enlisted me to gain your trust and make a deal."

"Sounds far-fetched to me."

"The last thing they wanted was for Nadia Ivanovich to escape with the technology, so the offer was witness protection, keep you in the country, and continue your work here."

She threw back her head and laughed; clapped her hands in applause. "Isn't it amazing how creative the human mind can be when placed under extreme duress?"

"All true. Not in my best interest to lie right now."

"Here's the problem: I don't believe you. If the FBI finds me now, I'll be arrested for what, espionage? Why? I haven't stolen any technology, haven't revealed any secrets."

"I'm your only way out."

"I appreciate the offer, but you deceived me once, and you won't deceive me again. So now I need to punish you. I will leave you here to die of thirst and starvation, but I first have to punch back. Personality flaw of mine."

"The goal was to protect you, but you abducted three people—four, including me. Now the feds don't know what to think." She leaned against the workbench with her arms folded across her chest. "Keira. This is not going to end well for either of us. Get out of this while you can," I said.

"I'm tired of talking. I'll be right back. Don't move."

She went upstairs and made another phone call.

Eric, please. Triangulate. Do we have her number?

I never dreamed I'd go out like this. I always thought a bullet would drop me in the street. Some random punk in a stakeout gone bad, or a routine investigation that goes sideways. Never tied up, naked, in the basement of some house, at the hands of a deranged woman.

She would not believe anything I said, so I only had one choice and that was to attack: go on the offensive—thanks, Eric.

The call ended and she came back downstairs with her black bag over her shoulder.

I'm in trouble.

"Did you miss me?" she said. "You're almost right about one thing, though. This will not end well for you, because, unfortunately, you became a loose end." She took a .32 Beretta from her bag and held it up. "Nah, no fun in that." She put the pistol back in the bag and pulled out her stun gun and held it in front of my face. "Much more fun. It also feeds my addiction."

"They abandoned you. Forsaken by your own people. They should have exfiltrated you long ago with the technology, but you screwed up. Your handlers were unhappy with your affair with Bellamy and they turned their back. You have no way out. You became the loose end."

"Quite an imagination, Mr. Delarosa."

"True, isn't it? The irony is, I'm giving you a safe exit and you won't take it."

The once sparkling blue eyes turned to cold blue glass, as if her inner demon now came to the surface and transformed her into the monster she was.

She came close, looked me in the eye, waved the stun gun in front of my face, gave me a wink, and with one quick motion, stuck the gun under my balls...and fired.

The current of electricity shot through my body in milliseconds. My head jerked back as I screamed and my entire body shook in a violent tremor. Tears streamed down my face, mucus gushed from my nose, and I began an uncontrollable cough that ripped at my lungs and throat.

"My favorite part is watching the reactions. Most men curl up into a ball and scream. But I usually don't tie them up, so I rather enjoyed seeing you twitch and shake with no control over your own body."

The coughing stopped and my eyes slowly focused. "Katie. Where is she?"

"Who is Katie?"

"The girl who works for me, you sadistic bitch." I screamed and yanked the ropes, straining every muscle in my arms and legs.

"No idea what you are talking about. Maybe she ran away?"

"Where the hell is she!" I was out of my mind, livid, panicked, in pain. I pulled so hard the ropes cut into my wrists and blood trickled down my arms.

"I'll keep an eye out, and if I see her, I'll tell her you were asking for her. But, unfortunately, the next thing you'll see will be the rats waiting to have you for breakfast."

She slammed the stun gun into my groin again and fired.

My head jolted back in a scream.

Darkness swallowed me.

45

I awoke to a tickle on my right foot. The mouse sniffed at my toes. I shook my leg and he scurried off. The good news: I was alive. The bad news: I was still strung up and left for dead. My arms ached, numb, the blood drained; my groin burned and stung, my legs throbbed, the muscles stretched and strained.

My bladder must have let go. There was a puddle under me on the concrete, and it smelled like the floor of a gas station bathroom. Two mice would run out to the puddle, decide whether it was something they wanted, and then scamper back under the stairwell. Daylight appeared in the small window on the opposite wall. *Dawn? Did I hang here all night? Did I sleep or did I black out with the second shock?* I could not believe she didn't kill me, but I realized she was killing me. She hung me out to die and let my body rot. She was right: the rats would devour me before I was found. I figured I had two days left. So thirsty...my throat dry, as if I swallowed a bucket of sand. Two days without water would leave me weak, emaciated, and waiting in line for St. Peter.

Time to make my final confession? No, I decided. Not yet. As long as I was breathing, I had a chance, and the only thing I could do at the moment was the most important—I prayed.

My days as an altar boy at St. Anthony's flashed through my mind. I don't know why, but I remember it as a happy time. I had an active, healthy childhood in an Italian-American family and serving at Mass was both an honor and a privilege. I'm sure I grumbled plenty at having to serve the 6:30 a.m. daily Mass, but now I recited every long-forgotten prayer filed away in my memory.

A minute passed, or an hour. I don't know. I kept telling myself to think through the angles and work on a plan. Stay alert, think. Not the time for my brain to turn to delirious mush.

The sound of footsteps above me broke me from my ponderings. Two pair. One heavier than the other. They walked through the house, not talking. *Were my prayers answered? Were Quade and Ortiz upstairs, or was it the two Russians coming to finish the job?* The footfalls stopped at the stairwell, the door opened, and my heart pounded as they came down the stairs.

"Johnny, holy shit." It was Mike, with Eric behind him. Mike had his Glock in his hand. "What the hell—"

My throat so dry the words barely made it out. "Saw by the workbench." Eric found it and they cut the ropes and lowered me to the floor. "Oh Jesus. My arms."

"PI Dude, you okay?" They massaged my arms to bring them back to life. "Where's your clothes?"

"Water." It came out as a whisper.

"Eric, go up and see if you can find some clothes and water," Mike said.

"By myself?"

"Fine, here." Mike took a second gun from his ankle holster and handed it to Eric. "Anyone comes down those stairs and it's not me, shoot them. Try to find something to cover him up."

Mike went up the stairs. Eric rummaged through several of the boxes, finally finding a few bath towels. He knelt down and covered me with one and rolled another into a pillow. "You all right?" I shook my head.

A door opened and closed above us. Footsteps padded across the floor, lighter than Mike's. Eric looked at me, I looked at the gun in his hand, and tried to nod my head. He swiveled around beside me and faced the stairwell with the gun held in front of him.

The footsteps crossed the floor several times. All went quiet for a minute, then water ran through the pipes. Someone was in the kitchen or a bathroom. The steps resumed.

The heavy pistol shook in Eric's hands. I reached out with a numb arm and lowered his hands to the ground. If someone other than Mike came down to the basement, he had plenty of time to aim and fire.

"Hey..." A male voice upstairs...a loud grunt and a hard thud. Sounds of a scuffle...voices went back and forth...another crash. Then all went silent.

Eric inched backward until his body touched mine. If what happened upstairs went against us, he needed as much reassurance as possible.

The door at the top of the stairwell opened and Mike hurried down the stairs. "We got to get out of here." He had clothes with him and a bottle of water. He sat me up and put the water to my lips. "Sip it."

They pulled a pair of sweatpants on me and a T-shirt and squeezed my feet into sneakers a size too small. The water began to bring me back to life and they slowly helped me up. "How did you find me?" My voice was raspy, but it worked.

"The boy wonder here found Victor Mackey's name on a company that owns this farm."

"We're on a farm?"

"Thirty miles west of Port City. We took a chance, parked about a quarter mile down the road and walked up. We watched the blonde go into a big garage behind this house."

"She took a stun gun to my balls." Both men recoiled back as though I were contagious. "I need to kill her."

"First things first, partner."

"She has a weapon, too," I said. "Katie and Mary Ann got to be here somewhere."

"My guess is the garage," Mike said. "Here." He handed me a 9mm Ruger. My arm was so weak I could hardly hold it. "Courtesy of my friend upstairs. We go out the front and around to the left. It will put the house between us and the garage until we figure out an approach."

I nodded. "Quade?"

"Thirty minutes behind us. We called him after we saw the blonde. He was none too happy but he'll live. Enough talk. We got to move before they come looking for their man."

"Wait," Eric said. "I...I'm not sure about this. I never shot a gun before."

"Let's hope you won't have to, but if you do, aim for the chest and squeeze. Just don't shoot either one of us."

Eric's skin went pale, his hands trembled, and his eyes wet. "It...this is real shit...and—"

"Hey." I put a hand on his arm. "Stay beside me, do what we say, and do not make a sound. You'll be fine."

He nodded. I didn't know whether he would be fine or not, but we had no choice.

Mike led the way up the stairs. I was slow, one step at a time, my legs sore but moving. I stopped and glanced back at my torture chamber.

Yeah, I needed to hurt her real bad.

46

We huddled against the right side of the house—if looking in from the road. It was surrounded by a lawn and had a driveway that came in on the left side and wrapped around to the back. The garage was actually a modern cinder block barn with a corrugated metal roof, a roll-up door in the center, large enough for tractors and harvesters, and a standard door off to the side. Forty yards of open space separated the house and the barn, which would leave us exposed and vulnerable if we decided to approach.

Keira's Mercedes sat beside the barn and we could only assume she was in there with—I hoped—Katie, Mary Ann, and George. Mike incapacitated one Russian; where was the other—standing guard over the hostages? How many other comrades did she have with her?

"Now what?" Eric asked.

"Do not talk. We need to think," I said.

Mike was always the voice of authority in a crisis, with a command presence many of the men in blue learned to respect. I had been side-by-side with him many times in situations just as dangerous and he was a natural leader: bold, fearless, and rarely betrayed by his instincts.

"Partner?" I asked.

Mike shook his head. "Too open. No way to go from here to there without being seen. The smart thing to do would be to go back to our car and wait for the feds, or send Eric back and you and I find a spot to observe until Quade shows up."

"By myself—"

A *click-clack* interrupted Eric.

The all-too-familiar sound of a pump-action shotgun behind us. We spun around.

"The smart thing to do is to hand over your weapons and cell phones." George Ainsley had a twelve-gauge leveled at us.

"George," I said. "What are you doing?" George aligning himself with Keira did not surprise me, but him pointing a shotgun at us was a bit of a bombshell.

"Guns first." Eric tossed his immediately to George's feet, followed by his cell phone. "You two, c'mon." Even if one of us tried to squeeze off shot, his shotgun could easily take out two of us. Mike and I threw our guns and phones and stood, instinctively taking a step away from each other. Clumped together, we're one target; separated, we might have a chance. "Stop, right there, Delarosa. On the ground." I sat beside Eric. He aimed at Mike. "Pull up your pant legs."

He did, and revealed the empty ankle holster on his leg. "The gun is at your feet."

"Stand up, lift your shirt and turn around." Mike complied, showing no other weapon. "Sit back down." He made me and Eric go through the same routine, and when he was confident he had all our weapons and phones, he threw them all into the grass.

No doubt now it was George who gave up the safe house. *How deep was he in this? Were he and Keira partners?* I didn't buy it. I needed him talking and distracted. "Didn't take you for a tough guy, George."

"Life's full of surprises, isn't it?"

"This is a big one. Thought we were working together? Why don't we talk about this before you find yourself in real trouble?"

"Nope."

"Mary Ann and Katie, where are they?"

"You'll find out."

I noticed Eric's hands were trembling. That can happen the first time you stare down the nasty end of a barrel, unsure of the motivation or mental stability of the person with his finger on the trigger.

"George, you want to tell us what's going on here?"

"No talking. Stand up. Hands above your head. Walk to the barn. If any of you try to run, your girl Katie dies without a second thought."

He marched us across the open space and when we were close to the building, the door rolled up. The structure was cavernous and empty, except for the white van we'd been watching for the past two weeks was parked on the left side as we walked in, and against the opposite wall was a long portable table with two computer monitors.

Mary Ann and Katie sat on the concrete floor against the rear bumper of the van with their hands tied behind their backs. One of the Russians—no idea which one was now the guard and which one was dead in the house—stood over them with an automatic rifle.

The door closed behind us and Keira approached with Beretta in hand. "Well, Mr. Delarosa, I never thought I would see you above ground again."

"Frustrating when things don't work out the way we want, huh?" I turned to Katie and Mary Ann. "You two okay?"

They nodded.

"Shut up and sit down." George pointed the shotgun at Eric. "Except you."

Mike and I sat cross-legged on the floor and the Russian tied our hands behind our backs with some twine, pulling so tight it cut into my already bleeding wrists. "A little snug, don't you think?" He gave me a shove and knocked me over. I kicked out at him but he stuck the rifle in my ribs.

"You sure, Mister Superman?" he said in Russian accented broken English.

I got myself upright. Mike's eyes scanned around the building and I could tell he was assessing and calculating every option. The girls were about twenty feet to our right. Eric stood, trembling, his face ghost-white. His eyes begged at me for help.

George said, "We caught a break, Keira. This is the hacker kid I told you about."

She faced Eric and jammed the gun under his chin and put her other hand on his shoulder. "How serendipitous. Isn't that how you say it, a fortunate accident or coincidence. If you're the hacker George says you are, you just might save your own life."

Eric's brilliant computer skills kept him alive in prison. I hoped he would snap out of his fright and do the same here.

"I need to open a file, but it's password protected. Can you do it?"

He nodded. She grabbed his arm and led him to the table, but he stopped. "If I open the file, you'll let us go?"

No Eric, no time for negotiations. Do what she says.

She smiled. "Aren't you cute." She tousled his hair with her hand and then stuck the gun into his ribs. "No, if you open my file, you might live another day. I haven't decided about your friends." She shoved him into a chair, then tucked the Beretta in the back waistband of her jeans.

Two lap tops were on the table, along with four monitors, plus Keira's black bag sat beside her on the floor. She stood behind him and gave instructions.

I whispered to Mike. "George." He knew what I meant. In any hostage situation with multiple captors, there was always one weak link. Keira was the smart one; the Russian was too stupid to have an original thought. Which left Ainsley. He was our leverage. From everything I learned about Keira and Bellamy, she played him. Had to be.

"So it was you and Keira the entire time?" I said. "Certainly fooled me. I thought you were mad and jealous of Tom and Keira being lovers, but you outsmarted us all. She's a beautiful woman, too. Not bad, old man, scoring a woman forty years younger than you. Best sex you ever had, right?"

"You don't know what you're talking about, Delarosa." George took a stand in front of me and Mike. "Not even close."

"Why the change of heart? You hated the two of them. Now you side with her?"

He shook his head. "It was me and Keira from the beginning. We developed the program. Tom only got in the way. When they were together, I felt betrayed. It was when you had me in the house that I decided to take back what is mine."

"You forget she almost killed Mary Ann while trying to kill you."

"She had nothing to do with that."

Keira turned around. "Shut up, George."

"So you gave her the location of the safe house and got two men killed and two more wounded." I hoped a bit of taunting would dislodge him. "What's the plan here, George? Hold us hostage—then what?"

Keira marched over and grabbed his arm. "Keep your mouth shut, and stay focused." She kicked me in the ribs and knocked me over. Pain seared through my left side and I stayed down on the concrete, teeth clenched, telling myself to breathe through the pain. Anything we could do to disrupt the scheme would benefit, even taking a kick in the ribs. I heard Katie's voice and opened my eyes.

"Did that feel good, bitch? Huh, did it? Johnny, they're waiting for Tom Bellamy to call with the password. That was their ransom demand."

I righted myself only to see Keira headed for Katie. "Touch her and I will kill you."

It only motivated her. She struck Katie on the side of her face with an open palm. "I dare you to say one more word." Katie fell over into Mary Ann's lap and her sobs echoed through the barn. Keira came back stuck a finger in George's face. "Stop talking."

She went to Eric at the table and I looked over at Katie. Her head was still down, but I caught her eye. She sat up, whispered to Mary Ann, and began to cough. Violently.

Mary Ann struggled, but got to her feet. "She's getting sick. You hurt her."

The Russian aimed his weapon at her. "Sit down."

"She needs some water."

"I'm going to puke." Katie choked out the words between gags and coughs.

Mary Ann stepped forward. "Let me find her some water. Please."

The Russian moved closer and jabbed out with his rifle. "Sit down. Now. She is fine. No water. So what if she is sick." He pushed her back to the floor.

I yelled, "She needs a drink, you bastard." As the Russian turned away from the girls and headed for me, Katie stuck out her foot and tripped him, sending him sprawling. Mike rolled and got his feet under him, launched his body, and landed all two hundred and thirty pounds on the Russian's head and neck, causing a loud *snap*.

I scrambled around, managed to get up—and threw myself into George. He fell hard on his backside, firing the shotgun as he went down. The deafening blast filled the building, followed by a piercing scream.

I got to my knees. Keira was on her back, holding her right side. She screamed, "You idiot. You shot me." Her hands held her side as blood soaked her blouse and seeped through her fingers.

A few yards behind her, Eric was flat on his back, not moving. *Oh, Jesus, no.*

I checked Katie and Mary Ann—they were back to back, untying themselves. Mike made his way to Ainsley and put a heavy shoe on his chest to pin him down.

Katie was free and ran over. "The gun in her waistband. In the back," I said.

She crouched beside Keira and pulled the pistol out from under her. Keira swung out at her, but Katie gave her a shove that resulted in a long, agonizing scream.

"I'm shot," Eric yelled, and I was relieved to hear his voice.

"Eric, don't move," I said.

Mary Ann untied me and Mike, who ran to help Eric. I had Katie hold the gun on George, and told Mary Ann to find a phone and call 911. She dug the Russian's cell from his pocket. "Tell them to connect you through to Scott Quade with the FBI," I said.

Mike had pulled off his shirt and used it as a compress to put pressure on Eric's chest. "Need an ambulance, too."

George crawled to Keira. "Honey, honey, don't worry. We'll get out of this. It was an accident and you'll be fine. I'll take care of you and we can start our own firm, just like we planned."

"Shut up, you old fool. There is no you and me."

"What...what are you talking about...of course there is. It was our plan from the beginning...I know I let you down, but I made up for it, didn't I? Tom is the one who will pay, not us."

"It was never you and me, don't you understand?" She looked up at me. "Will you get this idiot off me?"

Mary Ann pulled George up to his feet. "C'mon, Uncle George." She sat him on the bumper of the van. Pain etched across his face. Her words hurt him more than any stun gun would.

I took off my sweatshirt, balled it up and gave it to Keira. "Hold this on your side."

I went to Mike and Eric. "How is he?"

"I think the bleeding has slowed but I'm worried he's going into shock. Any water in here?"

There was a slop sink in the corner and I found a few rags and soaked them. We put them on Eric's head and face and it brought him around a bit. From what I could figure, when the Russian went down, Keira and Eric must have headed our way, only to be caught in the spray from the shotgun blast.

I took the pistol from Katie and she ran to help Mike as I went to the computer table and took Keira's stun gun from her bag. I called for Mary Ann to join me and we stood above Keira.

She saw the stunner in my hand and her eyes went wide. "What are you doing?"

"I found it in your bag. How serendipitous."

"Nyet, please...please."

I held it out to Mary Ann. "She caused you a lot of pain."

She hesitated. "I...I don't—"

"Let me show you." I shoved the stun gun into Keira's crotch and gave her a shock she'd never forget. Her thin body flopped around and she curled up in a ball, screaming.

Mary Ann winced, stepped back, and looked at me as if I were a monster. "I owed her that." I held the device out to her. "Your turn. It will feel good. Trust me. Touch it to her skin and press the button."

"You sure?"

I nodded. "For you and George. You deserve it."

She took the gun and bent down to Keira. "This is for my sweet uncle." She touched it to her neck and fired. A long, low guttural moan filled the building. It sounded like a wounded animal who had gone off to die. "And this is for destroying my family." She shocked her a second time. Keira let out a grunt then went silent.

Mary Ann stood, her chest heaving. "You're right. That felt damn good. Can I keep this?"

"All yours."

I had no idea where we were, Mike said at least thirty miles outside the city, but it seemed as if it was taking forever for help to arrive. We took turns keeping pressure on Eric's wounds. Keira began to stir, her body recovering from the shocks.

Finally, I heard cars outside and I opened the roll door. Quade hopped out of his sedan as an ambulance and two state troopers pulled in behind him.

"Hey Keira, your ride is here. And it's not Aeroflot."

47

Doctor Marisa Alvarez examined the fluid level in my IV bag and decided another round was in order, explaining I was dehydrated to the point of doing some serious damage and needed to stay in the emergency room of St. Helen's Hospital until she deemed me fit to leave.

"I came in six hours ago. Unless you put bourbon in the bag, it's time for me to go."

She smirked. Some people have no sense of humor. The EMTs transported me and Eric in the same ambulance. When we pulled into the hospital's emergency entrance, they whisked Eric into surgery and parked me in the ER, where the lovely Dr. Alvarez and a nurse bandaged my wrists and stuck an IV in my arm. I told them about the burns to my body and caught them looking at each other when I showed them the location. Embarrassing.

She hooked up a second bag and made some notes on an iPad. "You're not going to like this, but I want to look at your burns again."

"Any ugly men doctors here? You being attractive makes it all the more humiliating."

She ignored me and pulled the curtain around the bed, threw off the sheet, and flipped up my gown. She did her inspection then covered me.

"You came in here with the blonde woman and she has burn marks on her neck, same as yours. Judging from your injuries, my guess is something really bad happened to you."

I shrugged. *Lady, you have no idea.*

"Plus your blood screen showed traces of ketamine."

"Date rape drug?"

"Yep. A sedative, used for anesthesia years ago. Puts the person into a trance." I understand her curiosity, especially with the cops and FBI hanging around, but my gut told me to keep my mouth shut.

She got the message. "None of my business?"

"I own a bar, McNally's. Not too far from here. You should stop in some evening."

"Now why would I do that?"

"Free drinks?"

She smiled. "The nurse will give you some ointment to take with you. Put it on your burns and your wrists until they heal. Discharge papers when the IV bag finishes." She patted my leg. "Take care of yourself, Mr. Delarosa." She disappeared through the curtain.

"Hey, call me Johnny." I hoped the torture marks on my body would turn her on, thinking I was some secret agent. It always worked for 007.

Quade flung open the curtain and stood at the foot of the bed. "He's out of recovery and being moved to a room. They took a shitload of buckshot out of his arm and upper chest. Lucky to be alive. He caught the edge of the shotgun blast. The surgeon says he will be back to normal in no time."

"Prayers answered. I never intended for him to be this involved."

"I need an official statement from you."

"Tomorrow?"

"Sure. I'll come by the bar in the morning."

"Katie?"

"Sixth floor. Waiting for Eric to wake up. I told her to go home, but she won't leave him. I brought her food but she won't eat either. Mike and Katie saved his life. Doctor said he lost a lot of blood."

"I'll find her as soon as they kick me out of here."

"I want to say I'm sorry about the way everything went down. We needed more eyes on the park. My fault." He moved around the bed so he was next to me. "You went through hell. What an evil bitch. Shocking what happened to you." He bit his lip and tried to keep a straight face.

"Is that supposed to be funny?"

"We hoped you would make contact, but I guess you were tied up, huh?"

"Get out. If I want jokes, I'll go to a comedy club."

"Laughter's a stress reliever. Later." He smacked my foot and pulled the curtain closed as he left. I could hear him chuckling as he lumbered through the ER. Nothing wrong with a good-natured ribbing and I wouldn't live this one down for a while. Good thing I am not a cop anymore—the squad room would be filled with jokes about my shocked balls.

***

It took another hour for the IV bag to empty and for the nurse to complete my discharge papers and send me on my way. I stopped at the sixth floor nurses' station to check on Eric, and then found Katie asleep in a chair in the waiting area.

I nudged her shoulder. "Hey."

She opened her eyes and stretched her long body. "Oh, hi. How are you?"

"I'm fine, but I want you to go home."

"I need to be here when he wakes up. His surgery was successful. Did Scott tell you?"

"He did. Wonderful news, but he's going to be knocked out till morning. Nothing for you to do here. C'mon, let's go. You need food and sleep."

"No...I don't want him to be alone."

"You'll be back before he wakes up. The nurse told me he woke up in the recovery room and wouldn't stop talking, so they gave him a sedative." That drew a smile.

"As long as I am back in the morning."

We got to the lobby and remembered neither of us had a car. She rode with Quade from the farm to the hospital, so we called for a taxi and ended up at a late-night diner.

A waitress put coffees in front of us. Katie's eyes were rimmed with red, between tears, pain, exhaustion, and the past two days of hell.

"Scott told me what happened. Did she really shoot you with the stun gun?"

"Yes."

"Right where he said? You know..."

"I do, and yes, it was brutal. And humiliating. I have ointment." That brought another smile, but tears welled. "Katie?"

She wiped her eyes with a napkin, drew in a breath. "I did not listen. You said time and again that this job was real, not like on TV, that it can be dangerous, and the people we deal with are the worst. You told me to not confuse fantasy with reality, and I did. I thought this was the coolest job anywhere—a private eye, investigating, spying on people, figuring out their schemes, working with the FBI, and...we work out of a bar. You and Mike are the most amazing guys ever, but I can't do it anymore."

Her forearms rested on the table and her head hung. Tears dropped. I got up and slid in on her side and put an arm around her. She laid her head on my chest and sobbed. "The whole time Mrs. Bellamy and I were tied up, all I thought about was the black bag and the stun gun...never so scared in my life...and I never dreamed you were in the house and that she used the gun on you...and I thought Eric was dead and it was all my fault. I got him into this mess..."

"If not for Eric, they would not have found us. No doubt in my mind she would leave us there to rot. Me, anyhow. He saved the day, and he knew what he was getting into. Granted, he didn't think it would escalate to the level it did."

"Him lying there, blood everywhere...too real...Mike held his shirt on him to stop the bleeding, for God's sake...and I couldn't believe the amount of blood coming out of him. I'm not supposed to be involved in shootings...people being hurt. I should be in some lame office somewhere...like my friends with their boring jobs. Who am I kidding? I'm done, Johnny. I'm sorry, I can't do this anymore."

"Your thinking saved us. You distracted the Russian and set events in motion—"

"And what if George's gun didn't go off? Huh? That was just stupid luck. We would all be dead."

I didn't have much of a response, because she was right. Was it stupid luck? Maybe not. Quade and his men were on their way to the farm, probably resulting in some sort of standoff.

I threw down some bills and kept an arm around her as we left the diner and hailed a taxi. During the cab ride, I tried telling her how brave and smart she was, but it fell short. She needed time.

She agreed to crash at my place. I heard the shower come on so I poured two glasses of an expensive cabernet. I'm not too skilled in talking people through tough situations, but I knew I would need to give her time to work through the ordeal on her own. I wanted her to know that our lives as investigators were not all guns, violence, and death. Those were the exceptions.

The shower turned off and after ten minutes passed, I peeked in the bedroom and she was in bed, covers pulled to her chin, out to the world.

I took both glasses of wine out to the balcony and gently lowered myself into my lounge chair. I sipped the wine and let it travel through me to warm my insides. The events of the past two days played through my head: being drugged, tied up, tortured by Keira and her stun gun, and rescued through the ingenuity of Eric.

Keira was my Rosa Klebb, the Bond villain in *From Russia with Love*. Except Rosa used a knife that popped out of her shoe, not a stun gun. I laughed that a 007 reference would flash in my mind. *Maybe I was the one who confuses fantasy with reality? Or was it the wine talking?* At any rate, I had a big *I told you so* heading my way. Mike warned me to not get involved with the feds and I ignored him.

I finished the second glass of wine and thanked God that Katie, Eric, and Mike were alive. I said a prayer for George Ainsley, too. He was the real victim in this. Mary Ann would survive—she has a lot of years left—but George did not. The mistake he made would be an unfortunate blemish on a stellar career. I prayed the courts would go easy on him and see him for the brilliant scientist that he was. His mistake? He answered the seductive call of the siren—not the first man to do so, and he won't be the last.

I could not fight off sleep any longer so I went back inside, took a blanket from the closet and stretched out on the sofa and closed my eyes.

Katie was right. It was crazy luck that his gun went off.

Serendipitous.

48

"PI Dude!"

A young nurse with short blonde hair tended to Eric. "Erica, meet Johnny, my boss. The PI I told you about. Johnny, this is Erica, my personal nurse. Can you believe it, Eric and Erica. Fate, dude—fate. We're soul mates."

She was cute in her blue scrubs and smiled as she worked, amused by her patient. "We are not soul mates. We just met three hours ago. And I am not your personal nurse."

"Dollface, you felt it immediately, just like I did. What are the chances I am brought in here after a vicious gun battle, riddled with bullets, clinging to life, and the first thing I see when I wake up is your gorgeous blue eyes? PI Dude, look at her eyes."

Erica blushed and shook her head. "You weren't almost dead and the surgeon removed all the buckshot." Two IV bags hung from a rack, tubes snaked into his arms, and a machine monitored his vitals.

"I thought I was in heaven because an angel was looking down on me."

"I am an angel, and I might even show you my wings, but only if you behave. Now lie back and rest."

"PI Dude, I get a peek at her wings."

She faced me. "Is he always like this or is it the pain killers?"

"No, this is mild. He's usually quite talkative."

"Is it true he's in a band?"

"An amazing bass player in a smokin' hot band. He's also a world-class computer expert, and works for me as an undercover PI." Eric pumped his fist in the air behind her back.

She crossed her arms over her chest and turned to him. "Well then, I'm impressed."

"Angel—" Eric tried to sit up in the bed but a pain knock him back. "Whoa."

"Lie still." She checked the IV bags and adjusted the drip on one of the lines. "I'm turning up the juice. You need to sleep."

"Dollface, I wouldn't tell you any stories. I'm the real deal...and this guy, he's the most righteous dude on the planet."

"I'll take your word for it." She picked up his chart. "I'll be back." She stopped in front of me. "He was extremely lucky. He lost some blood, and most of the wounds were superficial, except for a few where they had to dig deep, but the doctor predicts a full and speedy recovery."

"Great news! He was a hero yesterday. No joke. If not for him, I wouldn't be standing here now. I owe him my life," I said.

"Wow, Eric, I am in the presence of greatness. A real live hero."

"Right and we need to celebrate...as soon as I'm out of here. Me and you...those gorgeous blues are sending me signals. You can't argue with fate."

"I don't date patients." She winked at me. "Make sure he sleeps."

She breezed out of the room and Eric yelled after her. "Ahhh, my pain just got worse. C'mon, me and you. A night on the town."

She popped her head back in the door. "Maybe. Stop talking." She disappeared again.

"Yes! PI Dude, she is my angel."

I stood at the foot of his bed. "Your angel is Katie. Stayed here until you were out of surgery and wouldn't leave until she knew you were going to be okay."

"Katie girl. Where is she? I want to see her."

"She crashed at my place but was gone when I got up."

The meds kicked in and his eyes closed. "She and Big Mike saved me."

"They did, computer dude. They did."

***

Scott Quade and Maria Ortiz were at McNally's when I got back. It was after two and the lunch rush was over. We squeezed into my booth and I gave Quade my account of the past forty-eight hours.

"We all admit we needed a presence in the park," he said. "I'm sorry you went through what you did. I feel responsible. I brought you into this."

"You didn't force me. Matter of fact, it was a bit of a rush. Could have done without the stun gun, though."

Ortiz winced. "As bad as it sounds?"

"Well, she stuck it in a rather delicate area."

"He has ointment," Quade said.

"We're back with the jokes? Maybe you want to help me put the ointment on my burns?"

"Yeah, Scott, why don't you help him?" She jabbed him in the ribs.

"Shut up."

Mike brought a round of beers and a couple baskets of chicken wings. "Right on time, partner. I was about to shoot an FBI agent."

"That's fine by me, but I want to know if anyone has heard from Katie," Mike said. "She hasn't answered any of my calls."

Quade pulled a basket of wings in front of him. "I tried too. She went through quite an ordeal and I'm concerned."

"Give her time. I'm happy to talk to her. Female to female, but she also needs to process it on her own," Ortiz added.

"Appreciate that," I said.

"My main dude, Eric. How is he?" she asked.

"Full recovery in store. He's flirting with the nurses and he'll have stories to tell for years," I said. We toasted to Eric and his brilliance. "What about Bellamy?"

"Can't stop crying," Quade said. "Told us how he fell in love with Keira. Thought she was his future."

"Charge him?"

"Not yet. Need to figure out if he was a victim or an accomplice. All we know for sure is he was an idiot."

Ortiz smirked. "Like most men."

Quade elbowed her. "Drink your beer."

"Ainsley?" I asked.

"Our real victim. It was the classic Russian honey trap. She lured him with sex and he fell hard. Single man, never had a relationship—she showed him some attention, promised him a life, and he lost his mind. Still deciding on charges. Even if he skips on any espionage charges, he did help orchestrate the assault on the house and the abduction of Katie."

"Keira tell you this?"

"She's singing like a songbird from her hospital bed. Scared to death of being sent back to Russia."

"She'll be dead within a week if she's sent home."

"If she's lucky. Early reaction from the State Department is to try to use her as leverage. For what, I don't know."

"If we keep her here?"

"Charged with espionage against the United States for starters. I'm sure she can make a deal if she gives up names. Russian mobsters, other active agents in the US. Two uniforms are stationed in front of her room until she is discharged, then we take her into custody."

"So the cold war is alive and well?"

"Never ended."

"What about Bellamy Space?"

"Department of Defense will step in and assess the damage, if any. Your boy Eric really is a genius. He opened the file for Keira, but he added some sort of a self-destruct mechanism. After sixty minutes, the file disappeared. He stumped our tech guys."

I shook my head in amazement. "I need to keep him on the payroll."

"Or we do."

The agents said they needed to get back to the hospital for another Keira questioning. As we got up from the booth, Quade pulled me aside.

"Does she have a boyfriend? Katie, I mean. I was thinking of asking her out. If you approve."

"First, I'm not her dad, and boy, you are slow. She gave you every signal."

"I'm kind of a meathead when it comes to girls. Women. She is...pretty, and I like her. She makes me laugh."

What is it about women that turns men to mush? This guy was well over six feet tall, chiseled like a Greek statue, and when he talked about Katie, he couldn't get a word out without blushing?

"She would like that. Call her. You have my blessing, my son."

"Thanks." He shook my hand. "I'm coming back here for beers."

"Only beers. I'm not helping you anymore."

"Deal."

I made my way to the bar and gently eased my burns on a stool, where Mike had a bourbon waiting. I wasn't there two minutes when Mary Ann Bellamy walked in. She put an arm around me and we embraced, then hopped up on the stool next to me.

"Want a table? You don't seem like the type who sits a bar."

"Never was, but now change is in order, Johnny."

"I hope positive."

"I decided to make it positive. What happened to me was something I never would have dreamed. Him having an affair was bad enough, but the woman was a Russian spy? Beyond belief."

Mike put a white wine in front of her. "Mary Ann, happy to see you're okay."

"Thank you. I'm glad you're okay, too. Can I ask a favor, though?" She pushed the wine to him. "Could I get—" She looked at me. "A gin and tonic."

"Yes ma'am. Coming right up." Mike took her glass.

"It is a new day," I said. "I'm impressed."

She smiled. "A difficult day, but I'll make it. I have my friends and my son to lean on. They'll get me through and I'll be fine. But I am here to thank you for what you did, and to apologize for creating all this mess."

I waved it off. "Not your fault. You did nothing wrong. Did Tom contact you?"

"They let him call me. He was all apologetic, says he is sorry, wants me to forgive him, and talked about us starting over."

Mike set the drink in front of her.

"And?"

"I'm the one who needs to start over. Katie and I were held hostage, you were hurt, the poor kid Eric was shot, my uncle was humiliated and ruined, other men are dead, all because of his recklessness." She took a sip of her drink. "Ooh, strong. Good, I need it." She took a second sip. "Time I took care of myself."

"I'll drink to that." We clicked our glasses.

"You know, in some bizarre way, something changed for me when I shot Keira with that stun gun. I've never done anything like that before in my life. It gave me some sort of... satisfaction...or empowerment that I have never felt before."

"It set you free, didn't it?"

"It sure as hell did."

49

"Katie. This is my last message. The incident at the farm was almost three weeks ago and Mike and I have sent you many messages. At the very least, we should talk about what happened. You were scared, but you did not act scared. You were brave, and smart, and strong. You and Mike saved Eric's life. If you decided this work is not for you and have moved on, I understand. I want you to know you always have a job with us. We want to make sure you are okay. We love you and we are always here for you. Johnny."

I sent the text message while I sat in my car in the parking lot of Joey Mac's, where Mike and I decided we needed to blow off some steam. Let someone else serve us for a change. The absence of Katie in our lives was tough at first. We loved having her around, her sexy physical presence—we admit we are still lecherous—but in a way, we grew to love her as a daughter, too. Neither of us had children so she filled that void. We became quite protective of her.

We missed her laugh, and her goofiness, and her non-stop talking—never thought we would miss that—and her zeal for the work, both in the bar and helping me. We even named the gourmet grilled cheese sandwich, The Katie. Mike got the hang of making it and it is now our best-seller.

Scott Quade gave up on her, too. He stopped by McNally's a week ago for a drink and asked for her. She never returned any of his calls. He figured the entire ordeal shell-shocked her to the point where any association with any of us brought her right back to that day. He might be right. I did not think it was healthy for her to not talk about it, and I'm not one for shrinks, but I would pay for her to talk to a professional.

I slipped my phone into my pocket and went into Joey Mac's. Mike sat at the bar and had a head start on me. I took the stool next to him and the loud, rotund, former police sergeant came with a bourbon and a draft beer.

"Boilermaker for my buddy." Joey Mac set the drinks in front of me.

"Thank you, my friend."

"Johnny, word is you got your chestnuts roasted."

I shot Mike a look to kill and he busted out with a laugh. "Is nothing sacred these days?" I said.

"No, what happened to you is too good to not talk about. I had to tell Joey." Mike raised his mug. "A toast to your chestnuts."

"I'll never live it down." I threw back the bourbon and lifted my beer and toasted with Mike and Joey. "To my chestnuts, may they only experience love and kisses from this day forward."

We moved the party to a booth in the back of Joey's bar where he, the quintessential raconteur, regaled us with stories from his thirty years in the department. We heard most of them a hundred times over the years, but nevertheless, we howled with laughter and told a few of our own. We sat, drank, and reminisced for over an hour when my cell buzzed.

I opened the phone. A text from Katie—a picture. The selfie she took of me and her when we first surveilled Keira and Bellamy at the Dark Side. Our cheeks were pressed together with wide smiles. It made my night. I showed Mike and we raised a glass to Katie and both proclaimed she would be back. I hoped.

I went one more round with my two police comrades—since the Keira job, Mike and I called each other comrade—then announced I was not paying for anything. Joey proclaimed my money wasn't good there anyhow. I got up and we mafia hugged, Mike saying he had room for at least two more beers.

Joey whispered to me, "Don't worry, I have a cot in the back for him."

I got back in my car and my phone buzzed again. This time a voice mail from Brynne.

"Hi handsome, it's Brynne. I'm sure you remember me. I was thinking you should come by my place tonight. I thought we had...something, plus I need to apologize. Properly. Mary Ann told me what happened and I hope you are doing well. Anyhow, I'm about to make my world famous gin and tonics and I know you want one. C'mon over. I guarantee an evening you won't forget."

Oh no. If I was sober I would immediately press Delete. But I was not sober and the thought of her was inviting. Would it be a one-night thing and be over, or would she be the type to latch on and never let go? There it was: the call of the siren. The song that makes men lose all control of any rational thought and it now called me. I put the car in gear and headed in her general direction, unsure of my decision.

I went a few blocks when a crowd of people standing on a corner caught my eye. I slowed down and could not believe my eyes. They were all gathered in front of a club, the Pig Hole, a grunge bar that featured live bands. I drove around the block and stopped across the street from the club for a better view.

A banner hung above the entrance:

YEAST INFECTION
TONIGHT! ONE NIGHT ONLY!
GET INFECTED!

A smile shot across my face and suddenly everything was right with the world. I picked up my phone and looked at the picture of me and Katie. My heart was full.

I listened to Brynne's message again, and then pressed Delete.

I called Leah and she answered on the first ring. "Johnny, I'm at the beach house."

"I'm on my way."

AUTHOR'S NOTE

Space-based solar power is the ultimate in clean energy, and even though the technology has been around for decades, it is still in its infancy. Satellites can be launched into Earth's orbit with self-assembling solar panels that capture the sun's rays, convert it to electricity, and transmit the energy back to Earth via microwave or laser beam.

The obstacles? Funding a space-based energy program and transmitting the energy back to earth efficiently and safely. One satellite can supply enough electricity to power a city the size of Atlanta. But, unlike the scientists in our story, the ability to receive the power being sent back to Earth has not yet been perfected. Large receiving stations, called rectifying antennas, up to three kilometers in size, are needed to receive the space-power transmission, complete the conversion to electricity, and then upload it to the power grid. Much work needs to be done to reduce the size of the rectifying antennas and to safeguard the transmission of the space-power.

Governments are actively pursuing space-based solar power, notably, the United States, China, and Japan, along with many privately-held companies who hope to be at the forefront of a space-based clean energy revolution, all courtesy of our sun.

The technological information and research used in this novel has been collected from many sources, including government agencies, private companies, and scientific journals.

ACKNOWLEDGEMENTS

This book is dedicated to my parents, Evelyn and George Stever, two wonderful people who forever provided a warm and loving home, rich with tradition and wholesome values, and who continue to teach us with the greatest of example of how to lead a full and rewarding life with humility, grace, and unconditional love.

Thank you to Faith Williams and her expert editing of this book and for adapting to my ever-moving deadline! Brandie McCann again did a great job with the cover for the book. Much thanks! I am grateful to my brothers, Mark and Matt, for their nonstop promotion of my books. Thanks guys!

As always, thank you to my children, Brian, Kevin, and Cassidy, and to my wife Helene, for their never-ending love, encouragement, and support.

And a special thanks to my two new assistants, Lucy and Kent.

Johnny Delarosa
returns in:
Raven Rain
For more information, please visit
www.davidstever.com

Be sure to join the mailing list for
news, reviews, and updates!

Made in the USA
San Bernardino, CA
06 March 2020